MALLORY CAVAN
AND THE
MADCAP MUSEUM MYSTERY

BY

Jessica & Sophia Voloudakis

CHAPTER ONE

I lined up my shot and slapped it into the goal harder and faster than I'd ever done outside of a game. If there'd been a goalie in the net, he'd never have caught it in time. No way. As it was, Mr. Snuffles just yawned from his position near the stairs going up to my dad's back door. Mr. Snuffles was unimpressed by my killer shot.

So, as it turns out, was my dad. "Mal, if you want to make it to the next level, you have to get more lift on your shots. Come on. Try again—ten more times." His scowl, deep inside his red beard, made him look like an angry leprechaun.

I rolled my eyes and ground my teeth. Hadn't I been doing enough hockey for the day? Don't get me wrong. I love hockey. I've always loved hockey. It's kind of my "thing." It's just that I'd been at hockey camp until two, and now here on my dad's scorching hot patio for hours this afternoon. I love hockey, but I love other things too. Also, this whole *next level* thing gets on my nerves. It's not like they're going to put me on the high school team at eleven, right?

I took a deep breath and took another shot. I got a little more lift on this one, but it went wide and barely made it into the goal.

Dad groaned. "Come on, Mallory. At least *try* to hit your target."

My next shot didn't go into the goal at all. It did hit Dad in the butt though.

He pursed his lips, like he'd bitten right into a lemon and glared at me. Then he sighed. "Fine. Hit the showers, and we can talk about what you did at camp today." He headed toward the house. "Come on, Farley."

Mr. Snuffles got up and gave me a little nuzzle before following Dad into the house.

Farley is Mr. Snuffles' real name. He's my dad's K-9 partner over at the Black Sail Bay Police Department. He's a good dog, unless you're a bad guy, I guess.

I followed Dad inside, headed for the fridge, and got myself some water. People don't think it gets hot in New England, and here by the coast, maybe it doesn't get as hot as it does in some other places. I'm a hockey player. I spend my days on the ice. It was the middle of July and I'd been sweating for hours.

Dad sat down at the breakfast bar. "So what did your coaches have to say at camp?" He asked the same thing every day.

I shrugged. "Stuff. You know."

Dad folded his arms over his chest. "You spend five hours a day at that place and all they say is 'stuff'? What am I spending so much money for if you can't even remember what they're saying?"

I kicked at the floor. "You want me to record everything? I don't know. They said a lot of stuff. We did a lot of drills. We did shooting drills. We did passing drills. We did skating drills. We did a scrimmage. I sent the Scott twins into the boards—"

"That's not why you're there."

"That's exactly why I'm there." I drained my glass in one gulp. "Beating up on the Scotts is fun. If I do it in school, I go to the principal's office. You yell at me; Mom sighs and tells me not to get caught next time. If I do it on the ice, everyone laughs and tells them to up their game."

Dad scrunched up his face again. "I don't think you're getting the right messages here."

"I couldn't say. I'm not the one sending them."

He couldn't exactly argue with me, so he changed the subject. "So. Did they have any advice for you about lifting your shot?"

"Nothing any different from yesterday." I refilled my glass and drained it again. "Can I go do art now?"

He shook his head and sighed. "You're not going to get anywhere if you don't start taking this seriously. Fine. Go shower. Don't forget, we're going to your Nan's for dinner."

I forced a smile and fled to my room.

I did take a shower because I'd been sweating an awful lot. While showering was probably my second-least-favorite activity, even I had to admit I smelled kind of bad. Then I slipped into Bruins sweats and called my best friend Vivianne on video chat.

She picked up right away. She was out by the pool, of course. Sometimes, I was jealous of her pool, but she always let me come over. "Hey, want to come over? I think we're doing burgers and hot dogs for dinner!"

I groaned and buried my face in my hands. "I want to so bad, but my dad's making me go to Nan's. Again."

"Oh no!" Viv grimaced with sympathy. She'd been

out in the pool every day this summer, or at least every nice day. Her freckles had grown and were merging. She would turn into one giant freckle by the end of the summer, I was sure of it. "Is it going to be stew again?"

"Probably. I'm not sure she knows how to make anything else." I reconsidered. "There was that fish with the gross white sauce that one time. I'm pretty sure no one wants any part of that though. Not even Nan."

"Yikes. Has your dad thought about maybe just getting a backyard grill and cooking at home?"

I shrugged. "I'm not sure. I try not to ask. Only five more days until Mom's home though."

"And then you get to stay with her until school starts again, right?"

"Yeah." I found myself relaxing at the thought.

During the school year, I alternated weeks. During the summer, Mom went to Spain for half the summer while I stayed with Dad, and then I stayed with her when she came home. "I'm sure I'll be glad to come back to Dad's house by Labor Day, but right now I think I'm going insane."

Viv nodded. She knew me better than anyone else. She knew exactly why Dad and I rubbed each other the wrong way so often. "Well, I hope you survive dinner."

"Have fun with your cookout!"

I hung up and grabbed my sketchbook. What was Mom doing in Spain? I'd talked to her earlier today, but what was she doing *right now*? It was four here in Black Sail Bay, so it had to be ten in Seville. According to Mom, people tended to stay out late there. She was probably having fun with my aunts, instead of getting lectured by my dad about making it to the *next level.*

I started to draw. I wasn't even sure what I was doing, just getting some of my frustration out. Sometimes I do that, just sketching and seeing where my mood takes me. I found a hockey player—in a Bruins uniform, of course—taking shape under my hand.

She had long hair in a braid down her back, and even though I was drawing in black-and-white, I knew her hair was red. Her number was 8, my number, and she was faced off against that guy who used to play for Toronto before he cost his team the playoffs by being a giant jerkface. She dug her shoulder into his chest and sent him flying into a gigantic sign that said Next Level, smashing it to pieces.

After a couple of hours, I had a cute little comic panel going. It still needed something, so I added Mr. Snuffles peeing on the guy while he lay dazed on the ice. That made me giggle, and just like that, I wasn't so mad at my dad anymore.

By the time I was done, it was time to go over to Nan's.

My grandparents are good people. I love them, and they love me. They live in a condo development overlooking the country club. Grandpa was a police officer here in Black Sail Bay until he retired. Nan came over from Ireland to work as a nurse. They're very different people from my mom and me, but they love me and try to be supportive.

They feed us most of the time when I'm staying with my dad. I'm not sure if my dad ever learned to cook, or if Nan just thinks he can't cook. Either way, Nan isn't much of a cook herself. Mom says every time Nan cooked for her she used to get sick for a week. Dad says that's a mean thing to say, but he also admits it's true.

I've never gotten sick from Nan's cooking, but everything she cooks tends to turn out gray so I'm not exactly looking to push my luck either.

Viv had mentioned stew, which wasn't my favorite, especially in summer. I'd have been happy to have that instead of Fish Goo. The Fish Goo was some kind of fish—I had no idea what kind—and it was covered in some kind of suspicious white sauce. The same suspicious white sauce covered the unidentifiable green goo that was our vegetable. To give you a sense of what kind of horror lurked under the white sauce, even Mr. Snuffles wouldn't eat it.

And like all dogs, he eats poo.

Nan said grace before we could eat. I bowed my head. Mom told me once I didn't have to say the prayer, but I had to be respectful because it was Nan's house and it wasn't hurting me. I guess it wasn't a bad thing to say thank you for the food we're eating, or at least it wouldn't be if it were food.

Once Nan finished saying grace, she turned to me. "So, Mallory, how was camp? Were there any cute boys there today?"

I shuddered. I couldn't help it. Nan was always trying to find a boyfriend for me. I'm eleven. Sure, some of the girls I knew from school were interested in boys and romance. There's probably nothing wrong with that. Right now, it's not my thing. "Everyone wears face masks, Nan. We all look the same." It wasn't quite true, but it was close enough for her to understand.

And I'd said it yesterday, and the day before, and the day before that.

"Oh. I don't like that you're playing such a violent

sport. Aren't you worried you might get hurt? You should come down to the country club with us this weekend. There's a couple we play with; their grandson is coming to try the game out. You could meet him. I think he's a year ahead of you. Maybe you'll get along."

"Does he play hockey?"

"Well, no. He goes to Brightside Acade—"

Dad cringed, and I switched my grip on my fork. "I hate Brightside. They're a bunch of cheaters. And jerks. Do you know the ref didn't call a penalty on me when I tripped their forward last year because he was such a jerk?"

Nan winced. Grandpa gave me a very somber look. Dad covered his mouth to hide a laugh.

"You can't go around tripping people just because you don't like them." Grandpa nodded as he spoke. "You'll get in trouble."

I stared at him. "It's hockey. That's how hockey works."

Dad hid his laughter with his napkin now, which he then used to cover his plate. I noticed he hadn't eaten any of his dinner. Neither had Grandpa.

"Well, anyway." Nan continued like no one had said anything about tripping, the cheaters at Brightside, or hockey. "You'll come with us to the country club on Saturday and meet Sanderson, and I'm sure you'll get along like a house on fire." She patted my hand. "Golf is such a nice way to meet a husband, dear."

"I'm eleven, Nan. I'm too young to be thinking about a husband. And I'm way too young to be thinking about golf." I hurried to pick up the plates so she wouldn't notice none of us had eaten our dinner. "So tell me, did you try to get Dad into golfing at eleven?"

Grandpa rolled his eyes and started talking about my dad when he was my age. Grandpa knew what I was doing, of course. He winked at me as I brought our plates into the kitchen and scraped them clean into the trash.

I really hoped Dad would be willing to hit the drive-through on the way home.

CHAPTER TWO

It was about 12:30 when I saw Viv and her mom get to the rink. They stood out in the bleachers, especially Viv. Her hair was bright red, just like mine, but curly, and she had a ton more freckles than I do. (This is probably because she spends her days out by the pool instead of sensibly indoors on the ice like me, but why worry about it? We both look great.)

They took their places in the bleachers just as we got into position for our daily scrimmage. That was how we ended camp, every day, and I have to admit I loved it. I could live without the four hours of drills every day, but a full hour of game time, five days a week? Yeah, sign me right up for that!

I was faced off against Noah Scott, my eternal nemesis. We play on the same team, and we've played on the same team since learn-to-skate when we were in first grade. He's cocky, and a jerk, and I hate him.

"I'm going to score twenty goals off you," he told me, meeting my eyes.

I scoffed, after waving at Viv and her mom. "Please. You're not going to score twenty goals this season."

"You'd better hope I do. We're on the same team

again."

The whistle blew, and I won the face-off because Noah is a little twerp who would rather talk than skate. I barreled down the ice, knocking straight into three of the green team's defenders and sending them crashing to the ice. They only had one player I couldn't knock down—Will Redding, who was twice my size and knew how to use it.

I passed the puck to Samantha Holt, who scored by sneaking around Will while his attention was on me. Their goalie, Megan, cursed and then high-fived us both. We play together on another team, an all-girls club team, during the regular season.

Coach whistled for a line change, and I caught sight of Viv and her mom cheering. I had to grin. Only four more days until my mom was home, cheering right along with them.

Okay, I knew why Dad wasn't there. Mom's job was flexible. She wrote mysteries. She wasn't on the clock or anything. She could just put her laptop away, lock her house behind her, and come to the rink. Dad had to be out training with Mr. Snuffles or catching speeders or whatever else cops did. Still, when I saw the other kids' parents in the stands for these scrimmages and stuff and I didn't have anyone, it kind of bugged me.

And Viv, along with her mom Sarah, being here meant Dad wasn't going to be around after camp either. Dad had made arrangements with his boss to be home with me after camp as long as Mom was gone, but sometimes things happened. And when they did, he had to call people. Apparently today, he called Sarah McCrory.

I didn't let it get to me. I couldn't. Dad had to do

what he had to do, and so did I. At the next line change, I headed back out there and scored two goals just to make Noah Scott and his twin brother Logan cry.

Noah got one back though, which made me mad. He somehow got around me and scored while I was tangled up with his buddy. That made me see red, so the next time we were out on the ice together I made sure to send both him and Logan flying into the boards. Even Megan laughed at them, and she was supposed to be on their side!

The scrimmage went back and forth like that for a while. I won't pretend I didn't take my share of hits and falls, I just didn't complain about it. By the time the horn sounded, we were all laughing, and we all went off to change. Just as I'd suspected, Mrs. McCrory and Viv were waiting for me when I emerged from the locker room, big smiles on their faces.

"Hey, Mal!" Viv was all but floating. "Your dad's going to be stuck at work for a while. Him and Mr. Snuffles. He says it's okay for you to come over and hang out with us by the pool though!"

I grinned. Okay, sure, I was probably going to miss a call with my mom. That didn't exactly thrill me, but I hadn't gotten to spend much time with Viv this summer. Not because of anything bad, but because my dad likes to plan things out pretty far in advance and Viv's family likes to do things on the spur of the moment. "Sounds great!"

"Fantastic!" Mrs. McCrory ruffled my hair. "And hey, maybe the pool will get some of that hockey smell off of you." She lifted her eyes and looked at someone standing behind me. "Of course, you and your boys are welcome to come too, Alan."

I held back a groan. I didn't have to look to know

exactly who she was talking about. Only someone as unlucky as me could have a day with her best friend ruined with the most annoying twins on earth.

"I'm going to swim circles around you, Mallory." Noah growled the words into my ear.

I threw an elbow into his bony ribs. "You have way too much free time if you think that's a good way to spend a free afternoon."

His brother Logan laughed at him. Even his father chuckled as he thanked Mrs. McCrory for the invitation. "It sounds like fun—we'll definitely be there!"

The McCrorys didn't live far from the rink, and the Scotts had to drive home to get their swim stuff. That gave me time to change into my swimsuit—I kept one at Viv's place just in case—and gave us a few minutes alone together before the attack of the Terrible Twosome.

"I wonder what made your father have to stay late tonight." Viv hopped into the pool feetfirst, giving herself a good dunking. "Not that I mind—it's good to have you here."

"It's good to be here." I jumped in beside her. The water was a little too cold for such a hot day, but I'd get used to it quickly. "And who knows? It could be anything. Bank robbers, stolen car, lost dog."

Mrs. McCrory appeared with big glasses of water. She sat down beside the pool. "I think something happened at the museum. I'm not positive, but that's the rumor I heard."

I looked at Viv. She looked at me. We turned back to Mrs. McCrory and said, at the same time, "Museum?"

She laughed. "No wonder everyone thinks you're sisters! Yes, sillies, the museum. The Black Sail Bay

Museum? The town museum? You two went there on a field trip with your second grade class, and you got in trouble, Mallory, for punching Noah Scott in the nose?"

I ducked my head underwater to hide my blush. "He did try to pants me."

"It's true," Noah said as he and Logan appeared, running in from the gate to the outside world.

They wore only their swim trunks and didn't look anywhere before jumping into the pool with identical cannonballs. Fortunately, Viv and I had the good sense to grab our water glasses before the boys could knock them over or shatter them on the concrete patio surrounding the pool.

When Noah came up for air, he grinned at Mrs. McCrory. "It is true. I did try to pants Mal. But she was being a jerk."

"Telling you that Black Sail Bay wasn't founded by pirates and that you look stupid for saying it was isn't being mean, it's telling you the truth." I splashed him with a massive wave of water.

"But it was!" Logan recoiled. "Who the heck said it wasn't, anyway?"

"Er, were you paying any attention at all?" I blinked at him. "They literally showed us on that field trip. And, you know, my grandad's family."

"Oh yeah." He scratched behind his ear. "I forgot."

I didn't have a response to that.

Mrs. McCrory and Mr. Scott laughed gently, taking seats at one of the shaded tables near the side of the pool.

"Well, anyway, apparently someone stole something from the museum. That's all I know." Mrs.

McCrory shrugged. "I can't imagine what they'd have worth stealing."

"Or how anyone would ever know about it." Mr. Scott snorted. "It's not like anyone goes there unless they have to, for field trips."

"Right?" Mrs. McCrory stood up. "Can I get you anything, Alan? A glass of wine or maybe a beer?"

Alan followed her inside to see what they had, leaving us kids alone in the pool.

I grabbed a ball, and we tossed it around for a little while. "Actually, Viv, your mom was right. What would the museum have that anyone would want to steal? When we were there, it was mostly old, broken bits of pottery and farm equipment. Some stuff from old ships, but not anything worth money."

"Maybe it's about the pirate treasure." Noah spiked the ball right at me. "Did you think about that?"

"No, dingus. Pirates aren't real." I sent the ball straight at his chest. It knocked him back into the water, where he landed with a splash.

"They might not have founded Black Sail Bay, but they definitely stopped here. You can't pretend they didn't." Logan took a step backwards and held his hands up. "Look, it's a fact. This town was notorious for giving pirates a safe place to dock, so much so that they changed the name of the town. Didn't it used to be called Cheltenham or something?"

I made a face. He wasn't wrong. The town had finally given in and changed its name in the 1800s, but only because no one was willing to call it anything *but* Black Sail Bay. It was better than Chard, which had been the original name. "What's your point?"

"If there were that many pirates around here, there has to be treasure." He shrugged. "They're always going to want to unload that stuff somewhere—no one wants to have it go to the bottom of the ocean, right? Especially not with the way they were always firing cannons at each other and boarding each other's ships and making each other walk the plank and all that."

I hummed. When he put it like that, it almost seemed silly to think some of these guys hadn't hidden their treasure somewhere on shore. "Wouldn't someone have found it by now?"

"Dead men tell no tales." Noah cackled, one hand over his left eye like a makeshift eyepatch. "Come on, no one tells anyone where they're hiding the treasure. And hey, maybe someone did find it. Maybe that's what's been keeping the museum open all these years. Dad's right, it's not from admission."

All four of us nodded. No one would go to the museum if they didn't have to.

"But wait—if they put the stuff on display, people would come from miles around to see it." Viv grabbed a pool noodle and tried to sit on it. "Wouldn't that be easier for them?"

I sighed. "Maybe, but since when do adults do the easier thing?" I reached for one of the inflatable rafts. "Whatever it is, I'm sure Mr. Snuffles will find the thief before dinnertime."

"That would be a shame. We're having steaks." Viv winked at me.

"There's always paperwork." I laughed and then shrieked in outrage when Noah dumped me out of my float.

Revenge would be sweet and way more fun than arguing about pirates anyway.

CHAPTER THREE

Dad didn't come get me until nine, which made me feel a little awkward, but there wasn't much I could do about it. Mr. Snuffles was asleep in the back of the car when Dad pulled up, and Dad didn't have much to say when he came to get me either. He was snappish and short-tempered, to the point where Mr. Snuffles actually woke up and stuck his head in between us.

That woke Dad up a bit. "Sorry, Mal. I know I'm being a jerk. I'm tired and frustrated because work didn't go very well today, and I wound up running around in circles for too long."

I bit the inside of my cheek. I could understand that, I guessed. I don't like it when I'm doing something that seems to be going nowhere either. "Was it about the museum?"

He glanced at me. "How do you know about the museum? Have you even been to the museum?"

I rolled my eyes. "Duh. Field trips."

He snorted. "Don't sass. I guess that makes sense though. It's not like I didn't get dragged there for field trips when I was a kid too. Anyway, how did you hear about the museum? We didn't put out an announcement or anything. We've been trying to keep it hush-hush. That way, the crooks will think they got away with something." He glanced at me. "Makes them more likely to screw up."

I gave that some thought. "Sometimes we do that in hockey. You know, let them think they got away with something, and then we steamroll over them and score."

"Right. Just like that. Only with cuffs and jail time." He chuckled, just a little. At least his mood was improving. "So again—where did you hear it?"

It didn't take a genius to figure out that Dad wasn't going to let up. If he was being that insistent about it, it meant it was important. "Mrs. McCrory said she'd heard a rumor. But come on, Dad, you know she didn't do it. She'd have had to do it with Viv, and Viv would have told me."

Dad opened his mouth. He closed it again, and he pulled into the parking spot at his town house. "You're probably right. The two of you know everything about each other."

"It's true. We have no secrets." I jumped out of the car. Mr. Snuffles followed along with me.

"I still want to know where she heard something like that." Dad followed us inside. "So how was camp?"

"It was camp." I shrugged. "It was fun. I knocked down the Scott brothers a bunch of times. What got stolen from the museum anyway?"

"Never you mind." He shook his head and fell down onto the couch. "I should do a tick check. I spent too much time in the woods. I'm probably crawling with them."

"I hope not." I shuddered and then went to check Mr. Snuffles over. He's on flea and tick medicine, but you can't be too careful. Ticks are everywhere in Massachusetts. "Gina from school got Lyme disease, and she was sick as heck for a long time."

"Is that why you knocked her into her own team's bench the last time you played each other?" He raised his eyebrow at me.

"No. I knocked her into her own team bench because she called me a piglet, because I'm a cop's daughter, and because she stole someone's shoes and put them in Viv's locker." The penalty I'd gotten for that hit had been totally worth it too.

"Fair enough." He shrugged. "I should be more upset about it, but everyone knows about her. It says a lot that she's not allowed to play on the Black Sail Bay teams. Anyway, don't worry too much about the museum thing, sweetheart. It's not something you need to deal with. The most that will come off it is the museum using it to lobby for more funds from the town."

I made myself smile at him. I wasn't sure what *lobby* meant in this context, but it didn't feel right that he was just dismissing it. Dad was the most law-and-order guy I knew. The guy got irate about people driving two miles per hour over the speed limit, just because it was against the law. Him telling me not to worry too much about the *museum thing* just didn't make sense.

He also wasn't going to spill much to me in the way of details. Not right now, anyway.

I headed upstairs to my room and checked my messages. I didn't usually bring my phone to camp because it would be too easy to steal it, so I'd missed a call from my mom. It was too late now to return the call—it was four in the morning in Seville. Mom isn't someone you want to *wake up*, or speak to before she's had coffee. Not if you valued your life, anyway.

I sighed and brought my phone to bed. After a moment, I sent a text to Viv. A video chat request opened up a second later.

"What's up?" The freckles on her face scrunched together with concern.

I sighed. "Nothing. I'm just mad Dad made me miss a call from my mom. I mean, don't get me wrong, I'm glad I got to hang out."

"You just miss your mom. There's nothing wrong with that." She shrugged. "If you'd at least had your phone with you, you could have talked to her while you were at my house. You didn't get that chance. I'm sorry."

Something in my chest got all warm and fuzzy at her words. "Thanks, Viv. I don't know what I'd do without you."

"Rack up twice as many penalties as you do." She grinned impishly and sat back against her pillows. "It was kind of fun having the boys here, wasn't it?"

I made a face. "No, it was not. They're gross. Especially Noah."

"Noah's kind of a jerk, but Logan isn't so bad. Remember when he thought he was Wolverine?"

I laughed. "Just because his parents named him after a comic book character doesn't mean he *is* one!" I shook my head. "Listen, Dad's probably going to pester your mom about the museum thing."

She frowned, scratching the side of her head. "But she couldn't have robbed the museum. She was with me the whole time. And I'd have told you. You know that. We tell each other everything."

"I know, right? I told him that. But he's being all weird. Maybe he thinks she might know someone who *did* rob the place. I don't know why anyone cares. It's not like the museum had anything worth stealing. But he's totally acting weird about all this stuff, so I wanted to make sure I said something before he did something dumb."

She nodded, red curls bouncing everywhere. Adults did dumb stuff all the time. "I don't think she knows anything. I mean, everyone in town knows about it, Mal. Mom heard it from Miss Carina at the bakery. Miss Carina said she heard it from Ms. Wilson, the principal at the elementary school. And she's married to the museum director, Dr. Edwards, so you know she'd know the truth."

I frowned. "Yeah, she would. She'd have gotten it straight from the horse's mouth. But Dad said they're trying to keep it quiet." I ran my tongue against the back of my teeth. "What the heck? Why would Ms. Wilson be going around talking about it if they were trying to keep it quiet?"

"Grown-ups are weird and principals are weirder. Remember all those 'pep rallies' she kept trying to get going?" She rolled her eyes so hard I worried she might strain something. "It's like, we're in second grade, we don't have school sports, it's not something we have to worry about right now. It's stupid to sit there and shout GO TEAM when we don't have a team."

I winced and nodded. Ms. Wilson had always been a little odd. "Still, it's even weird for Ms. Wilson. Maybe I should say something to Dad."

Viv shook her head. "He told you not to worry about it. If you say something, he'll get mad. You know how your dad is. If he tells you not to do something, and you do it, he gets really mad."

"Isn't that how all dads are though?"

"Well, yeah. And most moms. But your dad's in the police. They're really serious about it. Let him ask my mom, she'll tell him the same thing I just told you, and he'll go talk to Ms. Wilson. Which neither of us ever has to do again."

"No, we've just got Dr. Crazypants Mitchell." I curled my lip.

"I like her! She's got clubs set up just for girls and helps me with my math."

"I'll help you with your math if you want. She told us that any hockey players showing up in her office have an automatic detention." I kicked against the mattress.

"Is that before or after the Scott twins checked each other into the lockers hard enough to dent them?"

"After. But they're brothers, it's different!"

"Not really. Remember when Eddie put Ethan *through* a locker?"

"Okay, but Ethan totally deserved it. Even Ethan admits it." I had to laugh at that one because Eddie's such a mellow guy. He plays bass in his spare time. Bass players are the most mellow people in the world.

"Sure, but they still had to repair the lockers." Vivianne was the eternal voice of practicality. "I agree with you. There's almost definitely something going on with the museum heist."

"Heist?" I chuckled.

"What? It was. Just because it doesn't have George Clooney in it doesn't make it not a heist—and anyway, you can't prove George Clooney isn't involved somewhere, somehow."

"Fair enough." I sighed. "So there's something weird about it, but we don't know what it is."

"And we probably won't." She yawned, big enough that I could see to the back of her tonsils. "We're eleven. We're going into sixth grade. They solve crimes for a living. We're kids. We're still learning basic stuff like reading. We're not going to somehow solve this crime for them."

I kicked at my mattress. "I know. I know! I just—I hate it when there's something going on and I don't know what it is. I always have."

"Don't I know it." She grinned at me, even though she looked tired. "You've always had to know everything, down to the last detail. Right now though, I don't think they're going to give it up." She yawned again. "Sorry, Mal. I think I need to go to bed now."

"It's okay. Thanks for listening to me." We hung up, and I looked around my room.

My room at my dad's house was pretty standard. It was girly, in ways I don't necessarily like, but the bed was comfortable enough for me and Mr. Snuffles to cuddle in and watch videos on my computer. My dad's parents had decorated it when my dad bought the townhouse after my parents split. They wanted it to be a surprise.

Hence all the pink.

The answers to the museum heist weren't going to be found in this room. They weren't going to be found in this town house either. Dad wouldn't want me asking questions, because he definitely didn't like me getting involved with his job.

The only person who did like me asking questions about stuff like this was Mom. She would probably have this whole case solved the minute she walked off that plane, but that was still days away. She liked it when I asked questions, not because it brought me closer to her job but because, according to her, it helped me to "stay curious, and keep everyone honest."

I had no idea what that was supposed to mean, but I really wished I could hear her now.

Mr. Snuffles nosed his way into my room and hopped up into my bed. I turned off the light and rolled over. Even I couldn't get all the answers tonight, but Mr. Snuffles could help me with the other problem just as easily.

CHAPTER FOUR

I was looking forward to a better day the next day because not only was it Scrimmage Day at camp but Viv's mom was dropping her off so she could come home and hang out with me all day. Mrs. McCrory and Dad had arranged it yesterday. Apparently, they'd brought the Scott twins in on it too, which didn't exactly fill me with glee, but I'd put up with it for the chance to hang out with Viv again.

And I guess the boys weren't terrible when it came to board games or whatever. I'd still rather play with Eddie or Mike from the team, but four usually made for a more exciting game than two.

We had a scrimmage every day at camp, but on Scrimmage Day all we did was scrimmages. It was my favorite day of the week. Viv's mom dropped her off after lunch, like they'd planned, and she cheered us on from the bleachers just as if she was my real-life sister.

After camp was over for the day, we went and changed. Then I met up with Viv and the Terrible Two and, in theory, my dad.

Except Dad wasn't there.

"He'll be here." I stood up straighter. "You know he will. He doesn't do the *late* thing." I wasn't just sticking up for him either. Dad had a permanent allergy to anyone being late for anything ever, which was probably the only thing he and my mom had in common other than me.

"He's probably stuck working on that museum thing." Logan curled his lip, just a little. "Didn't you watch the news last night? They're making a big scene about it. The museum owner said the thing that was stolen was, like, part of Blackbeard's treasure."

Noah punched his twin in the arm. "You need to read a book. Blackbeard was all about the Caribbean and the South—like, North Carolina. Not Boston and stuff. We had Captain Kidd."

Logan punched him back. "Blackbeard hid a huge treasure up in New Hampshire! Everyone knows that!"

"Prove it, you jerk!"

I glanced at the clock. Dad was more than twenty minutes late by now. "Look."

The sound of my voice was enough to stop the fistfight breaking out between the boys.

"It doesn't matter about the pirates, okay? We can't stay here, we're getting funny looks. We'll go home, call my dad from there, and tell him where we are."

The others glanced at each other, then back at me. Finally, they shrugged.

"Sounds good," Viv said. "You've got a key, right? We won't be breaking in or anything."

"I do." Dad had given me a key a year ago, and only because sometimes our timing missed by an hour after school, but hey—this was exactly that kind of situation, right? "He's been working hard lately; I'm sure he just forgot or something."

Lugging our hockey gear home was not going to be

fun. At least my bag had straps, so I could carry it on my back. The Scott brothers had to kind of rig something up with their duffel bags, which couldn't have been comfortable. I wouldn't have wanted to do it. It was probably less comfortable with them punching each other and continuing their fight about the stupid pirates, but whatever.

Black Sail Bay is *old*. The town was founded in 1638, and our path back to my dad's place led past some houses that were just about as old as the town itself. People here don't throw away anything if they can help it. That includes the buildings, I guess. We're not as big as Salem, or as famous, but that's okay. Mom says she'd rather get fewer tourists and skip the bad publicity of mass hysteria and murder.

It's easy to see the past here. We're proud of it—well, the good parts anyway. We put plaques on anything that existed before 1900, which is almost everything, and you can't tear down anything unless it's a clear hazard to public safety. No wonder everyone gets all misty about the days when pirates used to stop here—you can all but see their footprints on the cobblestone streets.

Those aren't original. No, we had normal pavement up until maybe 2002, when the mayor decided repaving them with cobblestones would attract more tourists. The town disability council still pickets that mayor's house, but the damage is done.

The thing is, getting from the rink to Dad's townhouse is a long hike if you take regular streets. If you cut through the woods, it's not far at all. Some people don't like to cut through the woods because they think the trees will eat them or maybe they think moss is contagious or something, but I've never had a problem with it. The town forest has stood there since before the first colonists set foot on this rocky ground. It's not something to be afraid of.

It's not like you get bears or anything this close to Boston.

I led my friend and the Terrible Two down a path I knew well, out of the harsh sunlight and into the shade of the town forest. Both of my parents had taken me in here, neither one knowing about the other one. Dad liked to point out things like ways to protect myself. Mom liked to point out historical features or unusual changes.

Today, I noticed both. My last visit had been before the end of the school year, toward the end of spring. It was mid-July now and the leaves were out in full force. All around me I could hear birds chirping. Mom had said they were mostly just warning us off, defending their territory like we were going to build nests in their trees or something, but it all sounded pretty to me.

People had been on this path. I didn't know who, but considering how close we were to the town center and the museum, it wasn't hard to guess. Dad says cops are supposed to avoid leaving traces behind, that they're trained, but it doesn't really work like that. I can see why it wouldn't. Broken sticks with heavy boot prints, little blue threads, brush swept away from random spots in the woods—all of it told me the forest had been investigated already.

"This space is creepy." Viv shuddered a little. "Why's it all swept away like that?"

I grinned. "Remember, the cops have been looking for evidence from the robbery?" I pointed toward a patch. "They've had to search the whole town forest. They didn't find anything though."

The twins looked at each other, eyes wide, and then back at me. "Cool!" They spoke with one voice, which was weird as heck, and tore up ahead of us.

"You did hear me say they didn't find anything, right?" I didn't run after them. I knew their hockey bags would weigh them down.

Sure enough, they slowed down maybe thirty feet up the trail.

"Okay, but grown-ups miss stuff all the time." Noah rolled his eyes at me. "And how cool would it be if we found the treasure for ourselves?"

I stomped my foot. "It's not *a treasure*; it's evidence. We can't keep it for ourselves, we have to turn it in. That's how it works."

"Oh, come on, Mal, live a little." Noah nudged me with his shoulder.

I elbowed him in the sternum. "No, that's really how it works. It's literally a crime to hide evidence. There's, like, jail time involved."

"So don't snitch." Logan scowled at me. "Not everyone's lucky enough to have a famous mystery writer for a mom."

"The only advantage there is getting a better lawyer." I headed back up the trail. "Come on. You can't honestly think they wouldn't find out. Logan, you couldn't even keep a secret about Rob's crush on Alyssa. You think you can keep a secret about something like this? And what are you going to do with the treasure? Pay for a new PlayStation with gold doubloons?"

Viv laughed. "That would be hysterical. How do you make change for that?"

Logan's face blushed scarlet. "We'd figure out a way."

"This is how they catch the bad guys in Mom's books *every time*—not because they're undeserving or anything, but because they don't think things through and they get caught doing stupid stuff." I could hear them walking behind me. "If you're going to do crime, you have to think things through. I'm not going to snitch, but you can't go telling on yourself like that."

"Okay, fine." Logan bit back a curse, and something hit the ground behind us.

I finally did stop and turn around. Logan was on his back on top of his hockey bag, like a turtle. He waved his arms and legs in the air, which made Viv giggle. She stepped in and help him though, which was nice of her I guess.

"Dude, what happened?" Noah took off his bag and crouched beside his brother. "Did you trip on a root?"

"Must have." Logan sat up and rubbed at his ankle. "It doesn't feel good, I'll tell you that much."

I winced and crouched down. I didn't *like* Logan, but I didn't want him to get actually hurt. For one thing, he was one of the better players on my coed team. "Do you think you can stand on it?"

"I don't know. Don't have much choice, do I?" He looked up at me with a grim smile. "I mean, I've got to get out of these woods, right?"

"We'll go get help if we need to." I turned to Viv and Noah. "You guys go to the end of the trail and get someone to call my dad. I'll stay here with Logan."

Noah's eyes widened, but he grabbed Viv's arm and nodded. The two of them took off running down the trail,

Noah's hockey bag abandoned with us.

Logan cursed again. "I'd better be able to play hockey. Dad paid plenty of money for this camp. And what else am I going to do all day, read?"

I snorted. "It could only help you." I glanced back at the trail. There were no roots anywhere in sight. What the heck could Logan have possibly tripped on?

I got up and walked over to the little disturbed patch of dirt where Logan had fallen.

He flipped me off. "Look, just because you're a bookworm doesn't mean the rest of us want to run around with our noses in books all the time, okay? Some of us *like* having free time and having fun. You should try it sometime."

I crouched down. "Reading *is* fun. Almost as much fun as knocking defensemen down while I score goals." I couldn't quite make out what Logan had tripped on.

There it was. Logan had stumbled on something sticking up in a bunch of loose dirt. I couldn't quite see why the dirt was loose. It could have been animals—that would make sense, considering the police hadn't dug up the spot and removed the obvious cloth and rope sticking out of the shallow hole in the ground. This had been what made Logan fall and twist his ankle.

"C'mere. Check this out."

Logan scooted over to see my discovery. "Holy crow!" He poked at the sack.

His sneaker had caused a tear in the fabric. When he poked, the tear opened up. I could see exactly what was in that buried sack. Glittering back at me in the partial sun were gemstones, a whole bunch of them.

Some of them, though, didn't glitter. Those were

covered in what looked like dried ketchup.

I swallowed hard and stepped back, bringing Logan with me.

"That's not ketchup, is it?" His tone was quiet, any trace of belligerence gone.

"Nope." I covered my mouth as a fly landed on one of the bloody gemstones. "I hope Viv and Noah get back with my dad *fast*."

CHAPTER FIVE

To say Dad was unhappy about my life choices when he showed up would be putting it mildly. He told me, right there in front of Viv and the boys, that I was grounded "for the foreseeable future." And he said it was my fault that Logan got hurt, because if I hadn't decided we should cut through the woods he'd be fine.

It wasn't Logan's fault for being a clumsy jerk. It wasn't the thief's job for doing such a lousy job of burying the bag or for stealing it in the first place. Nope. It was all my fault because I only waited half an hour at the rink for Dad.

Dad's supervisor, Lt. Ramos, finally intervened. "I think you've made your feelings known, Fred. We're not paying you to yell at your kid; we're paying you to deal with the crime scene. A crime scene your kid and her friends found when none of the rest of us did, right?" He caught my eye and winked. "I'll get statements from them, and then Mackey will release the ones who aren't yours to their parents."

Dad took off his hat and ran his fingers through his hair. It was red like mine, but a little more muted—maybe auburn, I don't know. "I'm supposed to be watching them all." He wouldn't look at any of us. "I agreed to it yesterday."

"Maybe you could have said something when you got in this morning, hm? Well, either way, we can't have a bunch of kids running around at a crime scene. You're going to have to call their parents. Why don't you go back to your squad car and do that, Fred. Farley and I can keep them out of trouble."

I sat down on the nearest rock, and Mr. Snuffles stuck his nose under my hand to ask for pets. I scratched his nose without thinking about it, but that little bit of contact made me feel a lot better.

Lt. Ramos shuddered. "You do know that dog chews through a two-and-a-half-inch-thick piece of copper pipe every day, right?"

I nodded, moving my hand up to my dog's ears. "He's such a good boy."

Logan paled. "Why would he eat copper? That can't be healthy."

"It's to keep his jaws in training and to practice sniffing for the things we need him to sniff for." Lt. Ramos grimaced. "Personally, Farley here scares the heck out of me. It's definitely weird to see him being all cuddly with Mallory. So tell me, kids. What exactly happened?"

Between us, we managed to get the whole story out, from the time camp ended to the point when Logan tripped.

By now another of Dad's coworkers, Officer Mike, arrived with a first aid kit and was wrapping Logan's ankle. "You should be okay, in a day or so, buddy, but I'd ice it when you get home."

"Thanks." Logan blushed.

I'd be embarrassed too, if I had to get my ankle wrapped by a cop in the woods.

"It's a good thing you had Mallory here to stand with you." Lt. Ramos glanced over at me with another grin. "Black Sail Bay is a safe community, but it's still not a great idea to be cutting through the woods by yourself—and definitely not if you're hurt. Did you kids see anything to suggest there might be something there?"

All four of us shook our heads.

"No. I mean we were arguing about whether or not it would be cool to find the pirate treasure, but we didn't think we'd actually find the pirate treasure." Noah swatted his brother on the back of his head.

"Everything looked pretty swept clean." I dragged my toe on the ground a little. "I figured it was from when you guys had been out here before. You know, doing crime scene stuff."

"You're probably right. I'm still annoyed that we missed it." Ramos scowled and glared back over his shoulder at some of the other officers. "Heck, I'm annoyed that Farley here missed it."

I cleared my throat and moved just a little, standing between Lt. Ramos and Mr. Snuffles. Lt. Ramos wouldn't *really* hurt an animal, but I wasn't taking any chances with my favorite companion. "Er, well, there was blood on the bag, but it was buried, right? So maybe whatever was on top of the bag, under the dirt, kept him from picking up on the scent. Except it did attract an animal, like a raccoon or something. That would be how enough of the string got dug up to trip Logan."

"Can we stop focusing on me tripping?" Logan tossed a clump of dirt at the back of my leg.

Noah nudged him with his knee. "Can you stand up? No? Then quit talking."

Lt. Ramos laughed. "I think that's quite a theory, Mallory. It's a tactic we haven't seen in Black Sail Bay, but I've heard of similar things happening with other K-9 units. Where did you hear about it?"

"My mom was researching for one of her books, and she brought me along on a demonstration for the Customs beagles." I blushed as red as my hair. "I know it's only mystery books—"

Lt. Ramos held up a hand. "No, no. I know your mom does a lot of research for those books—and the Customs beagle program is pretty awesome. You're right. Something smugglers sometimes do is hide the contraband—like drugs or a food item they're not supposed to bring into the US like cheese—in something with a strong scent like coffee. Sometimes it works, and sometimes it doesn't. That's really good thinking, Mallory. I'll make sure the lab tests the bag holding the items to see if that's what they did." He ruffled my hair as he turned to face my dad, who was coming back down to the scene.

Dad glared at me again and patted his thigh twice. Mr. Snuffles sighed and went to Dad, ready to get back to work.

I couldn't be mad, not about that. Mr. Snuffles was a working dog, after all. He had a job to do.

There weren't any real new clues to find, but my dad and his coworkers worked hard to make sure anyway. They even dug little pits anywhere they thought the dirt looked even a little bit disturbed. My buddies stayed with me until their parents came, but they couldn't exactly hang around and try to back me up.

I'd have even accepted one of the twins, if it meant I didn't have to deal with my dad alone.

It wasn't the first time I've had to sit and wait while my dad worked. Crime scene work looks exciting when you see it on TV. I'm here to promise you, it isn't. It's a lot of sitting around while a bunch of adults poke at the ground. I didn't have any books with me. I didn't have my phone with me, or we wouldn't have been in this situation to begin with. I was hungry, because I'd just been at camp all day, and I was thirsty.

And I smelled bad, because hockey.

Finally, sometime after six, Lt. Ramos called it. "I think we've exhausted the possibilities here, boys. Fred, take your kid home and get some water into her. And don't be too hard on her, okay? She did find us our only actual clue in the case."

Technically, it had been Logan, but I wasn't going to fight him about it. Especially not if it got me out of trouble with my dad. Plus, I couldn't help the little jolt of excitement that ran through me. Was this really their only clue?

I could see it now. *Sixth Grader Mallory Cavan Solves Major Mystery.* It would be the most amazing headline in Black Sail Bay history. Mom would be so proud of me, she'd frame the front page. She'd mail copies back to her family in Spain.

Dad was happy to burst my bubble as soon as the doors to the squad car closed. "I wasn't kidding about you being grounded basically forever." He buckled his seat belt and pulled out of the parking space. "I can't believe you were that irresponsible. What were you thinking?"

"I was thinking we couldn't sit there at the rink

anymore." I crossed my arms and looked out the window. "We'd been sitting there half an hour, after getting changed, and we needed to leave. None of us had phones, none of us had food, we needed to leave. I had a key. What would you rather I'd done?"

"Borrowed the rink phone."

"They don't let people use their phone, remember? Last year, Matt's mom's car broke down, and her phone was dead, and they wouldn't let her use the phone. They're definitely not going to let me use it."

"Did you try?"

"Why am I going to try when I already know the answer?"

He slapped his hand on the dashboard, making both me and Mr. Snuffles jump. "Damn it, Mallory, you have no idea who or what could have been in that forest. You could have been killed. Your friends could have been killed. Your one friend *did* get hurt, and all because you couldn't be bothered to ask someone a question? How selfish can you be?"

The accusation hit me like a puck to the ribs. "I just told you why that didn't make sense. Are you even listening?"

"Are you? You could have been killed!"

"And if we'd just loitered around the rink, they'd have kicked us out and we'd be having the same problem!" I was screaming now.

My face felt hot, like I'd spent the whole day in the sun, and I balled my hands into fists. I wasn't going to punch my dad. I wasn't that stupid. Right now though, I could definitely see the appeal.

"Don't you raise your voice at me, young lady." He

turned on the radio as loud as he could and refused to turn it down until we got back to his place.

He made me give him my phone when we got home and my tablet. "You're truly grounded. No screen time, no TV, nothing. You earned it. You're lucky you're not getting pulled out of hockey camp after a stunt like this. No more hanging out with Vivianne after camp. You're going to camp and coming right home, straight to your room for the rest of the summer."

I bit my tongue. I could argue with him. I could point out just what a colossal jerk he was being. There hadn't been any other way for us to get home, we hadn't been able to contact him, and that was just all there was to it. But Dad had already proved he wasn't listening to me, not now and not at any point in the future.

I kept my mouth shut and stomped into my weirdly pink room and closed the door most of the way. It didn't take long for Mr. Snuffles to push his way in. I let him climb into my bed, and I held him for a very long time.

Then I started packing.

Dad could take away my electronics if he wanted. I couldn't do much about that. And he could ground me. He and Mom didn't typically go against each other when it came to rules or whatever, so I'd probably still be grounded when Mom got home.

But at least I wouldn't be stuck here, in this room, for the rest of the summer.

CHAPTER SIX

The local TV stations were all at the rink the next morning, waiting for us. Waiting for *me*, I should say. Viv was there with her mom, and of course, Logan and Noah were there with their dads. Lt. Ramos was there too, and he stared Dad down when we got out of the car.

I didn't have to be a rocket scientist to know why the cameras were there.

"Fred, these nice folks heard about these kids and their find. They'd like to interview them all together. Mr. Scott and Mrs. McCrory are willing to sign the papers. Will you?"

I kept my hands on Mr. Snuffles. I didn't want anyone—especially the Scott brothers or my dad—to see them shaking. I wasn't sure how I felt about being on TV, but I didn't want to be the reason the others didn't get to be up there either.

Dad's jaw twitched. I'm not sure how that's supposed to work. I mean, a jaw is bone, right? But it twitched anyway. He couldn't say no to his boss. "I'm not exactly thrilled about Mallory being rewarded for doing something she knows a lot better than to have done, but it seems my hands are tied. Fine. She can be part of the interview." He glared at me. "Don't go thinking this gets you out of being grounded."

I nodded. "Can Mr. Snuffles be in the shot?"

"You call him Mr. Snuffles?" Lt. Ramos shook his head. "I don't have a problem with it if they don't."

"As long as his handler is there, we should be okay." One of the cameramen eyed my dad, a little dubiously. "He *is* a real K-9, right?"

"Oh, he is. He still likes Mallory better than Fred though." Lt. Ramos chuckled, and we got to business. After all, we still had camp to get through.

The press conference was weird. Two of the reporters seemed to think our brains were made of pudding, and two of them were kind of cool. One of the cool ones—a Black woman I'd seen on the news once or twice at my mom's house—asked why the police hadn't picked up on the clue when they'd swept the woods for clues before.

Much to my surprise, Lt. Ramos gave me full credit. "Mallory actually figured that one out for us. Don't get me wrong, I was plenty steamed about it at first. But she remembered something she'd learned about other K-9 enforcement programs, and we did some testing and figured out that was what was done here. The thieves hid the stolen property in something that was strongly scented, so it threw Farley here off—but it attracted other animals, who weren't trained to ignore the stronger-smelling food. They dug for it, which left it exposed for the kids to find.

"A lot of people like to underestimate kids. They think kids don't listen, don't hear, don't pick up on what's going on around them. And sure, kids don't always process things the way adults do—but they are smart, and a lot of the time they'll notice things adults don't because they haven't learned to write it off yet. These four really should be applauded. They figured out what had happened. When their buddy got hurt, they didn't leave him alone, but used the buddy system to get help. They did everything right, everything we could have wanted. They didn't even contaminate the scene.

"I'm proud of them, all of them—and I can't wait to see them on the ice when hockey season starts up again." He ruffled my hair, while I tried not to blush.

I'm not going to lie. I was flying for the rest of the day. Maybe Dad didn't agree with his boss, but Lt. Ramos had told the whole world that I'd done the right thing and that I'd even helped with the case. I felt like nothing could bring me down, not even a full day of drills.

Viv whispered to me before her mom took her home. "Did your dad really ground you?"

I nodded. "Yeah, for the rest of the summer at least."

She wrinkled her nose. "That's mean."

I sighed. "Yeah, well. He was scared."

What could I say? It *was* mean, but he's my dad. And he's a cop. He spends his whole day running around and seeing the worst the world has to offer, so of course he gets scared about things happening to me.

Dad went back to work, Viv and her mom left, and the rest of us got down to business. I barely noticed time flying by. Logan probably shouldn't have been on the ice, but it takes more than a twisted ankle to keep a hockey player down. The skates are pretty supportive, anyway.

Mom showed up just in time for the scrimmage. She looked amazing, like always. Her dark brown hair was maybe a little longer than usual, down to her collar, and the Spanish sun had blazed a few light streaks into it. Her skin was usually pretty light, but the sun had worked its magic there too and given her a beautiful tan. Her green eyes sparkled when she looked at me.

I'd missed her so much.

I rushed through changing after the game so I could get to hug her for the first time since June first, but I wasn't quick enough. When I got out, Dad was there. His lips were pressed into a thin line, so thin they barely looked like lips at all. Mom had narrowed her eyes at him in that way she had, the one that made most people wonder where the body would be found.

Mr. Snuffles trotted right over to me.

"Let's go." Dad turned on his heel and walked out.

Mom reached out and gave me a one-armed hug as we walked along. I could feel her tension as we walked, but she wasn't about to let me go without a hug. She scratched Mr. Snuffles behind his ears before taking my hockey bag from me. "My God, it's good to see you." She dropped a kiss onto the top of my head.

Normally, I don't let her give me kisses. I'm eleven. It's weird. But today, I didn't object.

We made it out to the parking lot. Dad's squad car was parked right next to Mom's Volkswagen. Mom popped the trunk, and Dad started loading my dirty laundry into it. "So like I told you, she's grounded for the foreseeable future. No electronics, no TV, no screen time. That's it."

Mom raised one eyebrow. "That's an interesting pronouncement."

"Look. I'm her father. It's right there in the custody agreement that whichever one she's living with at the time of the infraction gets to mete out discipline and the other one isn't allowed to undermine them. If I remember correctly, it was your scumbag lawyer—"

She held up a hand. "Don't forget the clause about nondisparagement of family members."

He closed his eyes as his face turned scarlet. "Fine," he said as his face went back to normal. "Your sister Clara, acting as your scumbag lawyer, put that clause in. You don't get to go back on it now."

"Well, there is that clause about 'just and reasonable' discipline." Mom's voice was sweet as syrup, which was never a good sign. "I'm sure we can always bring it up with a judge, if you'd like."

"Really? You want to relitigate the custody agreement?" He stepped closer to her, prompting Mr. Snuffles to move between them. A knot formed in my stomach.

"You're the one who brought the custody agreement into it." She shrugged. "I'm perfectly happy to leave you to your preferences at your home, provided you do the same." She smiled tightly. "Speaking of which, the clock is ticking. I've missed my daughter, and I'm sure you've got important work to get back to."

Mr. Snuffles pushed against Dad.

"Fine." Dad glared. "But I swear, Liliana, if you let her put herself in danger, so help me—"

"You're the one who didn't show up when he said he would." She raised her eyebrow again. "Don't make this ugly, Fred." She sighed. "Are you dropping Farley off tonight?"

"I shouldn't. But I suppose I will." He got into his car and drove off with Mr. Snuffles.

Mom relaxed once Dad was out of sight. She threw her arms around me and held on tight. "There. Let me get a good look at you. You've gotten even taller since I saw you last!"

I held on like she might float away if I let go. "Are you really not going to make me stay in my room?"

She snorted. "Look. Even if I thought you deserved to be grounded for what happened—and I don't—I wouldn't make you stay in your room with nothing. And I don't think he would either." She guided me to the car, like I'd get lost or something. I think she just didn't want to let go. "He was scared for you, and when he's scared, he reacts with anger."

"He's a big jerk." I slumped down in my seat.

"It definitely comes off that way. I don't think he should have treated you the way he did, and I told him so. I'm glad Sarah McCrory and Dave Ramos called and told me what happened before I saw him."

"They did?" I sat up a little straighter.

"Yeah." She grinned at me and ruffled my hair. "They both like you, and they wanted to make sure I had all the right information before I went into the conversation. And they like your dad too." She started the car and got out of the parking lot. "I'm so happy to be home, you can't imagine."

"You're not really going to go back to court?" I squirmed in my seat.

"I don't think I'll have to. I think he'll calm down once he has a little time and space to himself." She took a left, and I don't mind telling you it felt amazing to be heading toward her cozy old house. "So tell me about all this excitement that got you mixed up in police business in the first place."

I blushed again. "I wasn't trying to, honest. Someone robbed the town museum. You already know we were cutting through the woods to get back to Dad's house, and then Logan tripped. It's not that big a deal."

"Finding a bunch of gems is a pretty big deal, I'd say. And you weren't tempted to keep them?" She chuckled.

"No. I remembered how in every one of your books people do dumb stuff like that and that's how they get caught." I remembered something. "Hey, Mom. You know more about Black Sail Bay history than, like, anyone."

"I don't know about that. I know a lot about it, but our family's been here since the place was founded. We kind of accumulate little bits of information, like all that ugly china we found in Great-Grandma's attic."

I cringed. The stuff in Great-Grandma's attic had been a hideous mishmash of floral patterns covering centuries. According to Mom, she'd picked them up mostly at garage sales and flea markets.

"Were there really pirates here?" I asked.

"Oh, sure. It was kind of a problem. You hear more about pirates in the Caribbean because it's exotic and beautiful, while New England is cold and the people are kind of surly. We don't think of the Puritans as having much to steal. But piracy was a big issue around here—and local governments were happy to ignore them in exchange for some of their cash." She snorted. "The more things change . . ."

I had no idea what that meant, and if I asked, she'd go off on a tangent and explain. She might talk for hours. "Okay. So do you think the thing that got stolen was the pirate treasure? Because Logan thinks it's the pirate treasure, but I think if the museum had anything like it they could have bought real security systems or something."

"Hm." She pursed her lips for a moment. "Well, I definitely think there could be more security. But think about it for a minute. If the museum had actual pirate treasure, do you think they'd keep it quiet while they try so hard to get people to come visit?"

I shook my head. "No way. They'd never shut up about it."

"Then there's your answer."

If the museum didn't have any real pirate treasure though, what had we found out there in the woods?

CHAPTER SEVEN

We all went over to Viv's house again after camp the next day because it was hot as heck and because Mrs. McCrory and Mom wanted to catch up. It was different this time, of course, because Mom drove us all there and she sat with Viv's mom under an umbrella. Sometimes, she and Mrs. McCrory even got into the water, although they didn't really want to get in the way of our good time.

I'd still rather that Noah and Logan weren't there, but whatever. At least I wasn't locked in my stupid pink room in Dad's condo.

"Hey, Mal, is your mom's place haunted?" Logan splashed some water at me.

I rolled my eyes and used my legs to dunk him under the surface. "Is your face haunted? There's no such thing as ghosts. Just like there's no real pirate treasure at the museum."

He shook his head to dry it off, like Mr. Snuffles does. Mr. Snuffles is cuter though.

"What do you think I tripped and broke my ankle on, then? Macaroni and cheese?"

"If anyone could, you would." Noah checked his brother into the side of the pool. "And you didn't break your ankle, genius. You twisted it. You skated out the next day. It's not even swollen."

"But there was still a big bag of gems." Viv bit her lip. "There's a lot we still don't know, Mal, but it was a pretty big bag of gems."

I couldn't exactly argue with that. At least, I shouldn't. I had to find a way though because there was no way I was going to let one of the Scott twins be right. "So? That doesn't mean anything. It could have been put there by anyone. Mom said the museum doesn't even *have* a pirate treasure, and she's usually right about this stuff. If they had a pirate treasure, they'd have used it to get people in the door before now, instead of sitting around trying to make people look at the same stupid broken pottery over and over."

I'd found the right thing to say to get through to them, because they all nodded solemnly. Even Logan had to agree with that one.

"But the bag of gems still exists." Logan stroked his chin, like he was stroking a beard he couldn't grow yet. He was going to become one of those creepy goatee guys someday, I knew it. "So if it didn't come from the museum . . ."

"It must be pirate treasure." Noah rubbed his hands together. "You're right! There's a first time for everything, but you're right."

I looked at Viv. She looked back at me. "How exactly did you get from 'a sack buried in the ground' to 'it must be pirates'?" She looked back at me. "Are all boys obsessed with pirates, or is it just here in Black Sail Bay?"

"Like it or not, pirates were all over the North Shore." Logan jumped up onto an inflatable pool float and lay back. "And they had to do something with all that treasure, right? Why wouldn't they bury it? We saw it with our own eyes."

"And if it's not stolen from the museum, then it's finders keepers." Noah dove under the water and swam across the bottom until he got to the float. Then he sprang toward the surface and flipped his brother over. "We can do anything with that treasure, and we don't have to worry about hiding it from the police either."

Well, there went my argument against trying to find the stolen treasure. "Wait a minute—if pirate treasure wasn't taken from the museum, what was?" I scooted away from Logan's outraged flailing as he resurfaced. "There's not going to be treasure to find, just some moldy dead guy's cracked chamber pot."

We all shuddered. The docent who guided the school tour every year always insisted we had to look at the chamber pots. I'm not sure why.

"The police aren't spending days on end combing the woods for a chamber pot." Noah snorted. "Come on. There's something else going on here, and it could mean a lot of money for us."

"Nothing involving the police means a lot of money for anyone." I shook my head. "Trust me. It doesn't even mean a lot of money for the police."

"It means a lot of money for the lawyers." Viv piped up with that one. "My dad said that once."

"I should be a lawyer." Logan jumped back and kicked a bunch of water into Noah's face. "I want to make a lot of money."

"You'd have to learn to read first." I stuck my tongue out at him. "Plus, you have to go to school for a million years, and then you spend the rest of your life in a library. My dad was being a colossal butt when he yelled at me and grounded me, but he's right. We can't go poking around an actual investigation, on purpose. It could mean someone who's actually bad walks free."

"A chamber pot thief is a criminal mastermind now?" Noah jumped out of the pool and struck a comic book type pose. "Aha! I am the Poo Lord, thief of ancient toilet artifacts! No chamber pot on the East Coast is safe from me!"

Then he did a cannonball into the pool, splashing us all.

I laughed. I couldn't help it. Noah's a jerk, but sometimes he's funny. And he's not as bad as Logan.

"No, that's not what she meant." Viv was doubled over, she was laughing so hard. "But there was blood on those gems, wasn't there? If we go leaving our hair and footprints around it will make it harder to figure out who actually did the crime. And if they find someone and put them on trial, their lawyer will have an easier time saying, 'Well, you can't prove it was my guy who did it. Maybe it was one of these kids who did it, you don't know. Maybe the kids messed up the evidence of the real killer.' "

I nodded and pointed to Viv. "See?" Then I gave her a funny look. "Why do you know that?"

"Because I was paying attention when that crime scene technician your dad was dating explained it to us." She laughed. "I liked her. She was nice. What happened to her?"

"Oh. My Nan didn't think she was good enough." I rolled my eyes.

Nan didn't think anyone was good enough for her

little boy. She hadn't thought Mom was good enough either. I knew this because she told me.

"You know how it is. Anyway. That's why we can't go messing around with police work."

"Boring." Logan did a flip, something he could only do in the water. "Stop thinking about all the reasons why you have to say no and think about reasons to say *yes*, Mallory."

"You've been watching creepy horror movies again." I headed for the waterslide.

"We don't have to poke around with the museum theft. You say it's not the museum's pirate treasure, and you're probably right. That doesn't mean it's *not* pirate treasure."

"You're obsessed." I climbed the ladder. "You need help."

"The whole town is obsessed." Noah seemed to have gotten in line behind his brother, and Viv followed him. "It's like, the only way we get tourism here. We get a little from being a Quaint Seaside New England Town, but there's hundreds of them. We're the only one with pirates."

"Are not. Salem, Newport—"

"Not the point." Logan gave me a push, and I found myself going down the waterslide sooner than I expected.

I was going to get him back for that.

I splashed into the pool with as much of my dignity as a kid going down a waterslide can muster, and swam away before Logan could land on top of me. Noah followed, and then Viv.

"The point is," Noah continued for his brother, "that we could find the treasure. Ourselves."

"That's not interfering with police business." Viv tilted her head to the side.

"That's a technicality." I pulled Logan's little raft away just before he could land on it, making him splash unexpectedly back into the water. "I'm not doing anything that's going to make my dad lose his job. I'm mad at him right now, but I don't hate him."

"We don't want him to lose his job either. Which is why we're not going to mess with it." Noah put his hand on my shoulder.

I put the float between him and me. "No, you just want to go looking for more treasure."

"Which isn't part of what they're looking for."

"We can't be sure of that. The blood on that bag was fresh, Noah. I mean not fresh-fresh, but it wasn't hundreds of years old." I shook my head.

"Think about it this way." He stepped closer but didn't put his hands on me again. "Think about what happens if we do find the treasure, which isn't part of the museum theft. We can give the money—some of it, anyway—to the museum. They won't have to beg for funding. They won't have to drag school groups into the museum every year just to keep the doors open."

I ground my teeth. Somehow it still sounded like a bad idea. I didn't think the treasure had belonged to the museum, or had any connection to the museum, but *someone* had bled on those jewels. And someone had buried it, in a way designed to hide it from the police.

But if we *did* find the treasure and give it to the museum, Dad would have to admit I had the brains to think for myself. He wouldn't feel compelled to lock me in my bedroom if I came up with a solution to him forgetting to pick us up at hockey camp. He wouldn't sit there and threaten my mom with another custody fight if he wasn't worried that I was too stupid to find my own way home.

And, yeah, part of me was excited by the thought of just being one of the ones to find the treasure. It wasn't about the money. I'd liked it when Lt. Ramos got up there and talked about how I'd figured something out. I know Dad didn't *mean* to make me feel stupid, but it's what he did anyway.

And Mom? Well, Mom doesn't exactly make me feel stupid—any more than she makes other people feel stupid, I guess. But her dad's family were some of the first settlers to build Black Sail Bay. They've been here since day one and they've got a record of pretty much everything that's ever happened here, like it's just something that happened in passing. Now, Mom's part of Black Sail Bay's history, world-famous mystery author Liliana Corwin. Where am I supposed to fit in with all that?

If I helped find that treasure, I'd be a part of Black Sail Bay's history too. I'd be the girl who found the pirate treasure, one of the original Black Sail Bay Corwins. Mom would be proud of me.

"Fine." I still didn't like it. "But we're not going to do anything that gets in my dad's way, okay? I definitely don't want to get in deeper trouble with him."

"Me neither." Logan shuddered. "Not letting that dog bite me either."

"He'll only bite you if you say something stupid, I promise." I smiled as sweetly as I could, trying to mimic my mom's sugar-sweet fake smile.

"Dude, you're dog chow." Noah fell over, laughing and pointing at his brother.

CHAPTER EIGHT

Convincing Mom to let us go back into the woods was harder than I thought it would be. "Come on, Mom. It's not like there's going to be anything there anyway. Dad and Mr. Snuffles have been over the scene a million times. You can't think there's going to be anything else there."
She just shook her head at me. "That's not the point, Mallory. It's not the woods I'm worried about. It's just not a good idea."

I flopped down onto the couch. I liked her couch. The outside of her house was dark and old looking, but the inside was open, warm, and inviting. The couch was soft, and a girl could curl up with a good book for days. "You're not serious. Even the twins' dad is letting them go."

"I'm not responsible for the twins, and that's a good thing. Can you imagine?" She took a sip from her coffee and checked her tablet again. She frowned at something, fired off a quick message, and grabbed her coffee. "I know you want to go back out there and dig in the dirt, but it's a really bad idea for a lot of reasons. Most of those reasons have nothing to do with you, sweetheart. Why don't you just go over to Vivianne's and hang out by the pool? Or I can take you and Viv to the beach. You girls like that, even if I do get worried about sunburn."

"You don't get sunburns." I glared for a second, distracted by the colossal unfairness of inheriting my dad's skin.

"Not often, no. But I'm also careful about it. Your aunt Teresa is ten years younger than I am and looks like she's ten years older, and there's a reason for that." She raised an eyebrow. "How's hockey been going for you?"

"Good. I'm enjoying camp. It's better with you there." I pressed my lips together and buried my fingers in Mr. Snuffles' fur.

She shook her head fondly. "It's so funny to me that you and the dog have bonded so closely. I'm glad though. He's a good boy. Doesn't bother the cats. Keeps you safe." She tossed Mr. Snuffles a treat.

"So tell me, why can't I go look for the treasure in the woods?" Something clicked, deep in my brain. "You don't want to let Dad win, do you?"

She pursed her lips, just for a second. "Mallory, you know I can't say anything like that."

"It's not like I'm going to tell him." I heaved a huge sigh. "Seriously, Mom. After everything you said to him back in the parking lot, I can't believe you're just going to roll over like this."

"It's not rolling over." Mom rarely took a sharp tone with me, so it always seemed worse when she did. "We have a custody agreement for a reason. And it only works if we honor it. I'm not going to do anything ridiculous like lock you in your room for the entire summer because you acted reasonably under circumstances that were out of your control. That's ridiculous.

"But what I *do* have to consider, even if he's being

weird about it, is the fact that your dad has a lot of concerns about those woods. Any time the police investigate something, they have to keep parts of their investigation secret, right?"

I nodded. "Because they need to be able to weed out fake clues and stuff."

"Exactly." She beamed at me, and it was like the sun coming out on a cloudy day. I was the smartest kid in the world, at least for a few minutes. "So while it may seem absurd to me that he doesn't want you in the woods, I have to assume he has reasons he can't talk about. And I can back up that trust with the fact that *you* figured out that the jewels were hidden in a way that specifically hid them from Mr. Snuffles."

I opened my mouth to object. Then I closed it again. "Did I just nail my own foot to the floor?"

"Maybe a little, but you gave the police a huge clue. And I'm massively proud of you for that." She ruffled my hair, which I hated but somehow tolerated from her. "But if I sit there and ignore his concerns, then he has an easier time if I do wind up having to go to court."

I pouted for a second because I was still disappointed, but then I relaxed. "All this stuff is super complicated."

"It is. But you're worth it, Mallory." She reached over and grabbed me in a side hug. "And remember, he's doing it for your sake too. We both love you and always will."

I was obviously upset, but there wasn't much I could do. I peeked over her shoulder a little later and saw her texting with Mrs. McCrory, and decided to keep out of it.

My room at Mom's place is as different from the one at my dad's as night is from day. It's a little smaller, but I picked everything out there myself. The decor is mostly purple, with posters of my favorite Bruins and all the books and things I love. There are framed pictures of me and my mom, pictures of me and Mr. Snuffles, pictures of me and Viv, and pictures of me and the team.

I retired there for the night and dreamed of treasure. I'm sure my friends were doing the same thing. In my dreams though, I dreamed of solving the whole crime. I stood next to my dad and Lt. Ramos as the thieves—who had become little raccoons—got booked into the town jail. The museum added a little plaque next to a display about the pirates of Black Sail Bay about the theft, and explained how Mallory Cavan helped thwart the dastardly thieves.

The fact that the museum hadn't ever displayed such treasures, probably hadn't owned them in the first place, and that no one used terms like *dastardly* anymore didn't exactly cross my mind. But hey, no one controls their dreams.

The next morning, Mom greeted me and Mr. Snuffles with her signature tortillas españolas and orange juice. She had coffee, of course. "Well, the two of you will be thrilled to know that Sarah and I will be taking you all to the town forest today." She made a wry face. Mom was many things, most of them awesome.

None of them were "morning person" or "outdoor enthusiast."

I bounced excitedly for a moment, while Mr. Snuffles devoured his breakfast in seconds. Then I stopped.

"Wait a minute. Why the turnaround?" I took a bite.

Mom was a thousand times better at cooking than either Dad or Nan. I couldn't be happier that she was home, and for more reasons than I could count.

She slumped down into her chair. "Well, it's like this. After the story hit about you kids finding the rubies, there are more than a few people in the woods. So they're as safe as they can possibly be."

"There's got to be more to it than that." I was going to finish my food as fast as Mr. Snuffles, which was just embarrassing.

"Yeah. Sarah called your dad and basically guilted him into it. He agreed—eventually—as long as we went with you guys to 'keep an eye on things.' " She gestured at the can of bug spray on the table. "Hence the precautions."

I laughed. "Thanks, Mom. You're the best."

"I have my moments." She winked. "Eat up. Sarah is meeting us with Vivianne and the boys in an hour."

I raced through breakfast and the dishes in record time. Mr. Snuffles came with us, which required a backpack with water and Mr. Snuffles' harness. He wasn't wearing his police vest because he wasn't on duty, but we had to have it with us just in case Dad got a call.

Dad is the only K-9 officer in Black Sail Bay. Sometimes, he and Mr. Snuffles have to go to work at weird times. It's not much fun, but that's just the way it is.

For now though, Mr. Snuffles got to go and be a normal dog with me, Mom, my friend, and the Tagalong Twosome.

When we got to the parking lot for the town forest though, Mom's jaw dropped. "The whole thing is full!" She pushed a button on the touchscreen in her dashboard. "Call Sarah," she told her phone.

Mrs. McCrory picked up immediately. "Are you seeing this? It's packed!"

"There is no parking at all!" Mom accelerated slowly past our target.

My heart sank. There was no way we were going to get in there today. My visions of a plaque in the museum, of arrested thieves, danced out the window.

"There's a path into the forest over at the museum. That's how the thieves got away. Park there—you have a membership, right?"

Mom snorted. "I'm on the board." She sped up and aimed for the town museum.

"Of course you are." Mrs. McCrory laughed.

"I didn't know that." I turned to face my mom. "You could have told me."

"Why?" Mom gave me half a grin. "It's not a big deal. We meet four times a year to check in on the budget, which is tiny, and do drinks. I took your grandfather's place, and you'll take mine when I'm ready to be done with it. Assuming you come back to Black Sail Bay and don't make your home somewhere else, that is."

"Of course." I'd probably have my permanent home here, anyway, even if I signed with an NHL team. *When* I signed with an NHL team, because I was going to be the best forward the NHL had ever seen.

"Still, it could be relevant to the investigation." I shook my head. I was still going to be the best pro hockey forward ever, but right now, the theft was the most important thing in front of us.

She laughed gently. "You sound like your father, dear."

I shut up. But I wasn't happy about it.

We pulled into a Board Member Parking spot at the museum, and it's a good thing those spots existed because otherwise we'd never have gotten a spot. The place was packed, and it looked like most people were parked there to actually visit the museum too. That was probably good, right? People didn't usually think about the town museum unless they had to. The theft had changed all that.

Mom narrowed her eyes though, and I could just see the mystery writer at work. "Seems like the museum is benefitting an awful lot from this theft."

I did a double take. "Seriously? How is that a bad thing? They were the victims. Their stuff got *taken*, Mom."

"Mmm. Except it was stuff no one—to include the board—was aware they had." She shrugged and hooked the leash to Mr. Snuffles' harness. "Let's go see what there is to see, shall we?"

Mrs. McCrory texted her to meet up near "the old cellar hole," which apparently meant something to them because Mom knew exactly where to go and what to do. She led us to a pile of strategically arranged rocks around a small depression in the ground. A couple of rocks had some charring.

"How is this a cellar hole?" Noah wrinkled his nose.

I looked out at the rest of the woods. Any chance of finding anything out here was trashed. There had to be hundreds of people out here, stomping around in the underbrush, leaving their scent all over the place.

There was no way Mr. Snuffles would be able to identify a crime scene now, or any clues.

"There used to be a sign here, back when we were kids. The home apparently belonged to someone sheltering people considered 'Praying Indians' during King Philips'

War." Mom made a face. "The locals burned it down in a fit of spite and hate. Charming, really." She glanced away. "Well, it looks like no one's gotten to it yet. Why don't you go ahead and have at it? It's as good a place as any to look for clues."

We glanced at each other. Personally, I didn't want to get any closer to a place with that kind of history. Then again, it was as close to the museum as someone could get without being seen. "It's a good enough hiding spot." I stepped into the remains of the old cottage, repressing a shudder.

The others followed. We didn't find anything other than a couple of old nails, which the boys kept on the grounds of their cool factor, and the shed skin of a snake, which no one wanted to touch.

Then we went to one of the cafés in town for lunch—outside, because of Mr. Snuffles, but still. It was hard to eat, given what we'd just learned, but I was glad to get away from the old cellar hole. There was a lot more to Black Sail Bay than pirate stories. Why wasn't the museum interested in talking about that?

CHAPTER NINE

We met up on video chat the next day. It was Sunday, and normally, I'd be happy not to have to see either Scott twin's face all weekend, but I was in this whole treasure hunting thing to win it. They were part of the team whether or not I wanted them to be. I had to work with them. And, to be honest, both of them were pretty into the pirate thing. I could turn to Mom for real history, but when it came to pirates both of them probably knew more than anyone at the museum.

It hurt me to admit it then, and it still hurts me to admit it now. Don't tell them I said it.

"We should meet up at the library." It seemed like the most logical option to me, at least. Sure, the internet had plenty of information, but a lot of it was just nonsense people posted for whatever reasons of their own.

Logan scoffed. "You're such a nerd. Only a nerd would want to go to the library in the summer, on a Sunday."

"You want to come over here and say that to my face? Because you're the one who used to go around telling people you were Wolverine. You were even wearing stupid fake claws on a glove. In *school*." I crossed my arms over my chest and waited for him to remember why he'd stopped telling people anything of the sort.

Noah burst out laughing. "Mallory kicked your butt." He pointed at his brother.

"I think that glove is still on the roof of the school." I could see Viv trying to hide her laugh. She wasn't trying very hard, but I guess it was nice of her to try.

"Yeah, I guess. It was his fault for going near my eyes." I tossed my hair. "Anyway. The whole point is, there's nothing in those woods. If there were, all those people messing around in the woods would have found it already."

Something about what I'd just said bothered me, on a deep level I didn't understand. Still, I understood enough to make my point.

Unfortunately, so did Noah. "She's got a point. Pirates didn't exactly love going far from the water, you know? Their knees got all wobbly and stuff."

"That's a myth, dingus." Logan shoved Noah. "No one needs to get their 'land legs.'"

"How much time have you spend on a ship, spider breath?"

"That was one time, on a dare!"

Viv and I looked at each other with identical glances of disdain. *Boys.*

"Look. It doesn't matter about land legs or who ate a spider on a dare. What's important, if we want to find this treasure before any of the other people, is figuring out exactly where the pirates would have been and where people have looked and failed before." I couldn't understand why anyone would eat a spider, even on a dare, but I didn't want to get sidetracked.

"Way to sound like a TV show police captain, Mal." Noah stuck his tongue out at me. "You didn't even want to do this."

"No. I didn't. But since I'm doing it, we should do it right." I ground my teeth together. The dentist kept threatening to make me wear a mouth guard at night. I was starting to see where he might be right. "Look, we don't have to go doing stuff that other people have already done and gotten wrong, you know? We might as well let them make the mistakes. That's what grown-ups are *for*."

They all nodded, right there on my screen.

"Okay, but here's the thing." Logan gestured between himself and Noah. "Me and him, in a library? Never going to work."

Noah punched him in the shoulder. "You're making us sound stupid. It's not that we're stupid. I mean, Logan is stupid, but *we're* not stupid. But he's right, if we're sitting there in a library together and trying to sit still, we're going to break something."

Logan punched him in the shoulder. "I can sit just as still as any girl!"

"I see what you mean." Viv glanced over at me. "What if you and I go and do the research, then we come back and tell the boys what we found?"

I bit my tongue. I didn't want to get stuck with just me and Viv doing all the work while the boys got all the credit. At the same time, I could see where they'd get in the way. "Fine," I said after I got control of my temper. "But you guys do most of the digging."

"We can totally do that. We love digging." Noah smiled widely.

"We hate digging, birdbrain." Logan smacked his

brother again. "Unless we get paid for it."

"Fair's fair, fart face."

"All right." Viv spoke a little louder, to cut through the burgeoning argument. "We'll call you when we have something."

The boys cut out, and it was just Viv and me. "There's another reason I definitely don't mind getting rid of the boys." Viv bit her lip, and a little pink blush spread out underneath the constellation of her freckles.

"What's that?"

"Your mom knows how to do all this research. I mean we know how to do stuff for school, but your mom does this stuff for a living. And she makes, like, a ton of money at it."

I had no idea how much money my mom made, but she definitely made a comfortable income for us. "Sure. Okay. So?"

"She'd drown them. She's good with you, and us, but the locker rooms give her a headache."

It was true. Any time she had to come into the locker room or spend time with the team as a whole, she wound up sitting in a dark room for a while and needed a lot of quiet. "Okay. You've got a point. I don't think she's in the habit of drowning kids, but we do need her help more than we need them hanging around there."

She nodded. "Plus, we can't take the chance that she would kill your team's top scorer."

I couldn't argue with that.

Mom was willing to come and give us some direction in the library. "As far as I'm concerned, it's a matter of self-interest. Once you know how I do the research, you can take over part of my job." My horror must have showed on my face because she laughed. "I'd pay you, of course."

Pay made the whole thing different.

We picked up Viv and headed over to the library. Mr. Snuffles came with us. Library rules were pretty clear about the whole *no dogs* thing, but Mr. Snuffles was an exception even when he wasn't in his K-9 vest. I don't know if other patrons ever complained. He just stuck by me, and we were all happy with that.

Mom took us past the kids' and teen sections, up the twisting wrought-iron stairs that dated back to the 1890s, and up into a room so dusty Mr. Snuffles started sneezing. "Welcome to the local history and genealogy section. There are some internet posts that will give you a little bit of information, but it's incomplete and you don't know where it came from. Here, you'll find as much information going back as far as the original events, which will give you the clearest possible picture."

She led us over to one particular section. "What is it you think you need to look for?"

Viv and I exchanged glances. "Er, pirates."

"Seems logical, right? But here's the thing. People back then might not have seen what was going on as piracy. If Bill—sorry, William ye Mayor—had a side deal going with his friend Edward 'Blackbeard' Teach, then he's going to note it as a normal docking and normal business deal in his journal or whatever."

I scratched at a mosquito bite. This sounded a lot more boring than I'd hoped for my Sunday afternoon. "So no one was likely to have just written down, *ye buried treasure is here?*"

Mom tilted her head and looked up at the ceiling.

"Sure, it's possible. But if they had, someone would probably have found it by now."

We deflated, but we were already here. We might as well get to work. I went ahead and started digging into the records from around 1700–1710, and Viv took 1711–1720. Mom recommended we start with court records and import/export lists.

Court records weren't so bad. It turns out people got pretty weird back in the day. I found accusations of witchcraft, which were dismissed. I found a whole heap of cases about people making off with other people's wives, lawsuits about theft of crops and cattle, and people being punished in the stocks for falling asleep in church.

Seriously? Falling asleep in church was a crime?

The import/export lists were boring. I hated them. They were mostly numbers and lists of stupid things like bolts of cloth and sacks of sugar too. There were slaves too, which made me kind of want to throw up. I knew slavery wasn't just a thing that happened in the South, but having to look at those records made it all much more real.

It was those records, in fact, that gave me my first big clue. A merchant and a captain had a dispute about his cargo. I called Mom and Viv over to see the records. "According to this, the merchant Comfort White had commissioned Captain Thomas Shatswell—" We all giggled at the name—"to bring a cargo of tobacco, indigo, and slaves to Black Sail Bay from Charleston."

The weird language was hard to read, and so was the ancient typeface. I had to squint to read it, which gave me a headache. Still, if this gave me a clue, I'd do it. I could feel my heart speeding up, just like it would just before a game. This was it, I could feel it.

"Captain Thomas said he was attacked by pirates near Provincetown." I bounced in my seat. "He said the attackers took the indigo, the slaves, and all of the 'specie' he had on hand." I looked over at my mom. "What's specie?"

"It's a term for hard cash. So the thieves would have taken the gold and silver he had on hand. Is there a corresponding case in the court records?" Mom leaned over my shoulder and grabbed the right book.

It took me maybe ten minutes to find the right case. I should have guessed it would be there. Mom always knew that kind of stuff.

"It looks like there is. Comfort White brought a lawsuit against Captain Thomas." I couldn't make myself say the last name.

Mom took pity on me and took the book out of my hands. She had a lot more practice looking at this kind of typeface than I did. "According to this, Captain Thomas was seen digging in the dirt near the old light." She looked up. "There was a lighthouse over near where they built that breakwater, back in the colonial period."

"Why do you know that?" Viv just stared at Mom.

Mom gave her a wry smile. "There's a plaque there, if you look for it. The land belonged to my great-grandmother when they built it, and they had to put the plaque up there as part of the agreement." She chuckled. "I asked about it when I was your age. The first lighthouse burned in 1700, and they built a new one a little farther away. If you're smart, you'll start digging there."

I bit down on the inside of my cheek and buried my left hand deep in Mr. Snuffles' fur. "What happened to the enslaved people?"

Mom stroked my hair. "The court records don't say." She picked up the import/export list. "It does look like Captain Thomas made a voyage to Africa in that same year, returning without a cargo of enslaved people at the end of the year. It's reasonable to suspect he brought them back to where they'd come from. It's still early enough to think they probably came from there."

I relaxed for a minute. "But wait—was Captain Thomas a pirate?"

"Remember what I said before? Not everyone who was a pirate would be listed as a pirate." She winked at me. "One man's pirate is another man's privateer, and another man's naval commander."

I nodded, even though I didn't really get it. I guessed we had a place to dig, and that would have to be enough for me.

Just then, Mr. Snuffles started to growl. I glanced over at the stairwell, only to see the tips of someone's hair disappear as they fled.

CHAPTER TEN

I didn't really think much of the person who ran from the local history section. People have all kinds of reasons for going to that part of the library, and most of them are pretty boring if you ask me. They're boring, and they aren't always things they want other people around to see. Maybe they're looking into some deep, hidden family scandal. Maybe they don't want everyone to know they were looking to find a bio mom or something.

And hey, it wouldn't be the first time a fan was trying to catch a glimpse of Local Celebrity Author Liliana Corwin either.

So none of us worried too much about it. We just made notes about what we'd found and got out of there because no one wants to spend Sunday sitting around a dusty old library. Not even me, and I like books. We headed over to Viv's house to hang out in the pool, and then after Mom and I went home, Viv and I video chatted about our findings with the Scott twins.

We couldn't make it out to the beach until Tuesday because we needed to arrange things with parents and only Mrs. McCrory was able to take us there. Mom felt bad about not being able to go dig with us in the sand, but she had a book she needed to get out the door and she couldn't afford the time. I got it, even if I kind of wished she could be there.

The Old Light House was actually more recent than the records suggested. The first lighthouse, like Mom had said, burned down back before Captain Shatswell had gotten rid of his cargo. I knew where to look, more or less, and I led my friends over there. We had little hand trowels and buckets from the McCrorys' garden, and we were all pretty amped up to go digging.

It was pretty obvious right away that we weren't alone.

The four beachcombers stuck out like sore thumbs out here near the old light. Don't get me wrong, I wasn't expecting anyone to be out here in swim trunks or anything like that. The beach here in Black Sail Bay is rocky and kind of a mess. The town has put a lot of time and effort into making a safe sandy beach for people to use for swimming and stuff like that, but it's on the other side of the breakwater from where we were digging.

These guys though—I don't know about you, but I don't wear boots to the beach. And thick black jeans on a hot July day, in the blistering sun? For one thing, you're going to get them wet, salty, and sandy. For another, they're going to be uncomfortable when you sweat in them.

They just looked . . . sketchy. I know I shouldn't judge people based on how they look, but Mom says I should also trust my gut. My gut was telling me these guys were bad news. Maybe it was the way they all looked kind of like they hadn't washed up in too long. Maybe it was the dead look in their eyes. I don't know, but I didn't like the looks of them.

"Those guys over there are making me nervous." Mrs. McCrory fussed with the collar on her shirt, pulling it a little tighter around her neck as if it could protect her somehow.

The strangers gave us the stink eye too, almost as if we weren't supposed to be there. Or maybe as if we were the ones who were the threat, which would have been hilarious if it weren't so scary. I mean, we were a bunch of eleven-year-olds with a suburban housewife, what exactly were we going to do?

Maybe logic wasn't a thing with them. Maybe they had an allergy to preteens. Maybe they had a phobia of redheaded girls with freckles. Maybe they somehow knew we were hockey players and would mess them up six ways from Sunday.

"Here." I pulled Viv in for a picture. "Pretend you're getting a picture of us, but actually zoom in on them."

The boys absolutely had to get in on the picture because heaven forbid we don't include the Scott brothers in something, but whatever. It was a fake picture. "That's a good suggestion, Mallory." Mrs. McCrory took the picture, and a few more besides. "Where did you get the idea?"

I blushed. "Someone did it to Dad once. They showed up in court with pictures of him using Mr. Snuffles to search a car when he'd thought they were doing a picture of their buddies kissing." I recoiled a little bit at that because kissing was gross. "They had to throw out the whole case because the judge didn't think they should be searching the car."

"Well, it's brilliant." She put her phone back in her

pocket. "Let's do what you came here to do and get out of here."

She didn't have to tell us twice. I wasn't a fan of the looks those guys were giving us.

We got to work. The other guys were digging near the Old Light, so apparently they hadn't gotten the same information about the original lighthouse burning before Old Light was built. My friends and I exchanged glances and smirks. We were okay with them not knowing.

Each of us set up a few feet apart from the others, all in a line more or less in line with where the original lighthouse used to be. Mom had showed me on a picture of the site, otherwise I don't think I'd have ever found it. The only sign there had ever been something here was a few rocks with burn marks on them. I started digging at the end of the line, then Noah, then Viv, then Logan. I'd rather have been next to Viv, but we agreed to separate the twins because they'd just make a mess if we left them together.

When they started throwing bits of broken clamshells at each other, over Viv, we knew we'd made the right decision.

At first, we didn't find much. Logan found a beer can. Viv found an old pale-blue bottle that seemed to be more or less intact, which was pretty cool. We put that into a bucket. It probably had nothing to do with pirates or treasure, but it was still pretty cool. After an hour, we moved back a little.

Here, we did find some more interesting things. I found some rusty old nails and a couple of chunks of charred wood. Here, then, was what was left of the original light. Noah found some positively ancient bits of glass and more iron hardware that might have been left over when the place burned and collapsed.

In theory, we should have called the museum. We should have told them what we'd found, and let them call in some archaeologists or something. Right now, I didn't feel so comfortable calling the museum. They didn't have the best security, and while I wasn't sure just how someone would manage to steal a whole lighthouse, I was sure the museum would find some way of letting it happen.

So we didn't call, and we kept digging.

It was Logan who found the treasure. He didn't hit a wooden chest or anything like that though. I heard the unmistakable sound of a trowel landing on plastic—like my mom's never-ending supply of Tupperware. I tilted my head to the side and peered over.

Logan looked like he was going to shout in excitement, but his brother tackled him and covered his mouth with one hand. Apparently, he could see better than I could.

"Mrs. McCrory, you'd better call Mr. Cavan." He glanced over at Mrs. McCrory. Then he yelped and punched Logan in the face. "You little turd nugget, you bit me!"

I moved to screen them from the sleazy strangers' view. Now I could see what Logan had found, and I could see that Noah had been right to tackle him.

Someone had buried a modern container deep in the rocky, sandy ruins of the original lighthouse. And instead of gold doubloons or pieces of eight, or whatever passed for currency back in the day, they'd filled the Tupperware with crisp stacks of fifty dollar bills, neatly bundled with brown bits of paper.

I might be just a kid, but even I knew no one had

a legitimate reason to do that.

At best, we were looking at someone like Nan's brother Charlie. He lived in a special place for people with "memory care problems" now, but before he moved there he'd gotten a little weird and was firmly convinced the English were coming to take everything. He hid things in coffee cans and buried them all over the backyard. This *could* have been a situation like that, in which case the police would still need to be involved to figure out who the money actually belonged to and make sure the person was properly taken care of.

But, honestly, I didn't believe in coincidences. Finding this modern thing out here in the ruins, just when everyone and their mother was out looking for buried pirate treasure, was a little too much to be believed.

I could feel those weird people staring at us, but we managed to play it cool until Dad and Mr. Snuffles got there. It wasn't easy. My stomach was in knots the whole time, and I felt like throwing up. How embarrassing would that be?

Dad got there pretty fast, and he brought Lt. Ramos and a couple of other cops with him. They didn't have lights or sirens on, but as soon as those weirdos saw police, they made themselves scarce. I wanted Dad to go chase them down and bring them all in for questioning because you could tell just by looking at them that they were bad news, but that's not how things are supposed to work.

It's not illegal to go poke around on the beach, as long as you don't dig for clams without a license.

Dad fixed me with a terrible glare that told me he hadn't forgotten how mad he was about us finding those gems, and got the story from Mrs. McCrory. Thankfully, she didn't tell him that we'd done research and were actually looking for the stolen treasure. "The kids wanted to go out and see the beach. I don't know, I guess they were trying to play archaeologist or something." She shrugged. "But they found this, and since it clearly doesn't date back to when the original lighthouse was here, they knew enough to ask me to call you. I'd say that's pretty smart, wouldn't you?"

Dad glared at me again. "Oh, it's smart, all right."

Lt. Ramos nudged him. "Leave it, Cavan. Okay, you guys know you can't touch anything here, right?"

We all nodded. "Do you think it's drug money?" Noah swallowed hard. "We don't want to get involved with anything like that."

"That's smart thinking, kiddo, but we can't speculate about that. If we let ourselves make a story in our head about what this *might* be, we won't be able to see any of the clues for what this actually is if they don't back up our suspicions. Does that make sense?"

We all nodded, even though it didn't make much sense at all. We just didn't want him to explain further. That might take all night, and we didn't care. We just wanted to go home.

"Good. You kids did the right thing. We'll take it from here. You can head on home and enjoy a night off, right?"

Dad gave a sweet-as-sugar smile to Lt. Ramos. "I'll give Mallory a ride back to her mom's place, sir. I can see we've got a lot to talk about."

Ramos pursed his lips. "Fine," he sighed. "But you come right back here. It's pretty obvious we need you and

Farley here at the scene, not fighting with your ex-wife."

Dad saluted and turned back toward where he'd left his squad car. Before I went to follow, Lt. Ramos caught my eye and winked.

CHAPTER ELEVEN

Dad came over to Mom's house that night. He was mad, but he was calmer about it than he'd been when we found the bag of gems in the woods. "I don't believe for a minute that you kids just coincidentally wanted to play archaeologist. I don't think you even know what archaeologists *do*."

"Don't insult her intelligence, Fred." Mom sipped from her wine and gave Mr. Snuffles a treat.

Dad sighed. "Okay, fine. Mallory knows, but the Scott twins can't even pronounce *archaeologist*."

Mom and I both shrugged at that. It was the truth.

"Mallory, you can't keep sticking your nose in police business. We're trained. We have equipment. You're a child. You have a hockey stick."

"It's not illegal to go dig by the beach. You said to stay away from the woods, so we stayed away from the woods. I notice you didn't tell the *entire rest of the town* to stay away from the woods though, since literally everyone was there." I crossed my arms over my chest and flopped down onto the couch.

"They're not my kid. And if I had my way, I would tape off the entire woods."

Mom sipped from her wine again. "Fred, take a deep breath and think about this for a minute, would you? The thieves didn't go to the beach. They ran through the woods. Mallory and her friends stayed away from the crime scene, which is what you wanted—and is appropriate. The fact that they found evidence of a different crime is purely coincidental. They did the right thing when they found it then too."

"Except their digging and rooting around might have disturbed other evidence!" Dad smacked the wall, hard.

"They're children, Fred." Mom narrowed her eyes at him. Her voice got this chill I knew well. Grown men had seen their own graves when they heard that chill. "Crime scenes get disturbed by animal activity, by normal every day adult activity, even by normal natural processes like rain. The money could have been found by someone digging for clams. I know you're worried about her, and what she might have gotten caught up in, but you do *not* get to lock her away in some tower like Rapunzel in hopes that she never comes across anything that might relate to something tangential to your job." She put her wineglass down, which wasn't a good sign.

Mr. Snuffles whined and hopped onto the couch with me.

"Lil, you know there's no way that cash got there in a good way. You know it's drugs."

Mom turned her gaze over to me and Mr. Snuffles. "Mallory, why don't you and Mr. Snuffles head up to your room? It's late enough, and I know you're going to want to be at your best for hockey tomorrow."

Mom sending me to my room had nothing to do

with me going to bed, and everything to do with her wanting to fight with Dad without me watching. I headed off to bed anyway because both Mr. Snuffles and I hated to watch them argue.

I don't know what they said to each other, but Dad didn't speak when he came to get Mr. Snuffles in the morning.

Noah and Logan were pretty fired up about our find when we got to hockey camp the next morning.

"Dad says the money's from drugs. Does your dad think it's drug money?" Logan was so excited he could barely tie his skates.

I shrugged. "Yeah. I mean it's what makes sense. I'm not sure why they'd bury it out by the beach, but I'm sure it makes sense to a drug dealer. Whatever. It's not our problem. Dad and Mr. Snuffles will get the dealers and we'll go skate."

"I can't believe you're not more excited about this." Noah nudged me a little. "It's only the most exciting thing to happen in Black Sail Bay in, like, forever."

"We have drugs in Black Sail Bay all the time. Every town has drugs." I tugged my sweater over my pads. "It's not that exciting. Mr. Snuffles finds drugs every day. That's his whole job."

"I thought it was biting bad guys when they tried to run." Logan scratched his head.

"No, they try to keep that to a minimum." I grabbed my helmet and gloves. "Look, my dad's mad about the whole thing. Again. Let's just go skate, okay?"

"Your dad's always mad." Noah followed me. Logan was still getting suited up.

"He's not always mad, but this whole thing has him

all wound up wrong." I shrugged. "Something about the museum theft is rubbing him the wrong way, and it's making him grumpy. I don't know why."

I wasn't exaggerating that part either. I really didn't know why Dad was all up in arms about my having found things, or been around when things were found. Not knowing made it so much worse because I couldn't understand it. So it was bringing my mood down.

We hit the ice for drills, which were grueling today. Apparently, the coaches were grumpy too. That was fine, I'd show them and Dad that I could take whatever they wanted to dish out. We took a break for lunch, and then we broke up into teams for the scrimmage.

I hadn't been worried about the drug money we'd found. It was in Dad's hands and Lt. Ramos' hands. They were good cops, even if Dad was being a jerk right now, and they would solve the problem. We were just kids who found something. There wasn't any reason to come after us.

All that changed when I saw four men in filthy, salt-crusted jeans take seats on the bleachers just before the scrimmage started.

They sat down right in front of Mom. I could see, from the look on her face, that they stank. Had they been out all night? Why would they be here at the rink?

"Those are the creeps from the beach yesterday." Noah and Logan skated up to me and got close, so no one else could hear. "How did they figure out who we were?"

"I . . . I don't know." The words hurt. My heart was racing like I'd just finished a game. "This isn't good."

Logan glanced over at the dirty men. I followed his gaze, even though I didn't want to. Yesterday, all I could see was that they didn't look quite right. Here I could see more details. One had a long ponytail of dark hair streaked with gray. His eyes were light blue and colder than the ice under my skates. Another had a gross mustache and bad teeth. Another had scars I could see from center ice.

They didn't look like the kind of people I wanted to mess with.

"I don't think there's much we can do about them right now." I took a deep breath. "Let's focus on the game."

It was easy for me to say that. Doing it was something else. Those cold blue eyes kept following me all over the ice. I couldn't escape them. Every time I went back to the bench after a shift change, the smelly man stared right at me until I went back out.

It was probably the single worst game I'd played since I started playing hockey. I'd love to pretend I was cool as a cucumber and played like Brad Marchand out there, but I couldn't escape those eyes or how nervous they made me. It was like he had some kind of power to keep the puck away from me.

At least the Scott twins were equally bad. I wasn't alone in my shame.

After the scrimmage, we headed toward the locker room. I knew my mom would be there on the other side. If I could just get to her, it would all be okay. She'd do something—I had no idea what—and they'd run so fast they'd qualify for the Olympics.

My hands shook as I got out of my hockey gear.

Neither of the twins said anything as they got ready to go, but they stayed close to me as we emerged on the other side of the locker room in the broad, brightly lit lobby at the rink. Mom was there waiting for us, just like I'd hoped. We headed in her direction.

Four tall stinky figures blocked our way. This close, I could understand why Mom had made that face. These guys needed a shower, and that's saying something coming from someone who'd just been playing hockey for six hours.

"Well, hello, children." The guy with the blue eyes was the one who spoke. He had a bad Rhode Island accent, like nails on a chalkboard. "You found something that belongs to us. You're going to give it back to us. Now."

I scowled. I was terrified, but I was also mad. I dropped my hockey bag onto his foot. He shouted out a curse.

"Gee, Mister. What are you talking about? The only thing I've got is my hockey bag." I swung my stick, like someone who'd never seen a hockey stick before in her life, and connected it with his crotch. "Oh, and my stick. Oops!"

He doubled over, eyes blazing with rage. "You little brat!" he gasped, reaching out for me.

Noah picked up on what I was doing right away. He bent down to grab my bag, coincidentally smacking Blue Eyes in the face with it. "Mal, you dropped your bag!" He picked it up and swung it into the knees of one of the other creepers.

By now, Mom had made it over. Her phone was out. "What's going on over here?" She fixed Blue Eyes with that Thou Shalt Not glower she'd perfected over the years. "Who are you and what makes you think you can just approach other people's children like that?"

"Lady, these kids took—" This was the scarred guy. His voice was like gravel, and he reached out for my mom like he was going to put his hand on her arm or something.

"These kids took nothing but ice time, and so help me, if you touch them or me you will wish the police had better response times than they do." She smiled tightly.

"You called the cops because someone talked to your kid?" Gravel Voice gave her a funny look. "That's crazy, lady."

"I didn't." Mom pointed to someone in the crowd. "She did. And he did. And that person over there did. I don't know what you thought you were going to get away with, trying to intimidate kids at camp pickup, but we all know who's supposed to be here and who isn't."

Sirens wailed in the distance.

I hadn't realized we'd drawn an audience, but now I had the chance to look around. Every other hockey parent was watching, both the people picking up their kids and the high school families just arriving. A few people looked curious, but most of the adults just looked mad.

The creepers looked mad too. "You'll be seeing us again, and you'd best have our money when you do." Blue Eyes pointed at me. Then he and the others ran for the emergency exit. The alarm rang when they opened it, adding to the noise and confusion.

Dad and Mr. Snuffles didn't stop to chat. Mom told them where to go, and they ran after the creepers. Lt. Ramos stayed to take our statements, which was probably for the best. He wasn't mad or anything, but he was worried.

"These guys sound like bad news. I'm going to need you to come down to the station and talk to a sketch artist, so we can get people to be on the lookout for them. Are you kids willing to do that for me?"

None of us were going to object, even though it meant spending the rest of our afternoon in the police station instead of hanging out and playing video games or reading. Honestly, considering the number of police at the station, it seemed like the best place in the world to me right now.

CHAPTER TWELVE

To say Dad was mad would be putting it mildly, but Mom was right there by my side. She made it clear she wasn't going to let Dad start shouting, even though Dad's face was almost as red as my hair. "Obviously we need to have a talk about all of this, but we're going to do it while we grab dinner somewhere."

"I don't feel like Mallory's earned going out to dinner right now, do you?" Dad spoke through gritted teeth.

Mom raised an eyebrow. "Mallory was a victim here, and she handled herself very well under the circumstances. But going out to dinner isn't a reward. It's a way we can all talk about this without getting angry and arguing. This is something all three of us feel strongly about, and if we're out in a public place we'll be a little better about expressing ourselves calmly." She smiled sweetly.

Muscles in Dad's jaw twitched, and I realized everyone in the station was watching us. He couldn't say no without making a scene, or more of a scene than he was already making. "Fine." He took a deep breath. "But this isn't over."

"That's the whole point, Fred." Mom sighed. "We'll meet you over at Antonio's. My treat."

We'd spent a lot of time at the police station giving statements and working with police artists. I hadn't realized how hungry I was until Mom mentioned Antonio's. My stomach gave an appreciative growl, and Dad's whole stance softened even as he glared at me.

"Fine. Whatever." He whistled to Mr. Snuffles, who nuzzled my hand before following Dad.

Lt. Ramos turned to Mom, biting his lip. "Do you need me to come and play mediator? I know how he can get."

Mom shook her head, brown hair swinging. "We should be okay. We'll be in a public place, and I know what's driving it. We'll be okay. He's worried, not just lashing out because of job stress. He's already had his work and home life mixed a little too much for comfort right now. Thanks for thinking of us though."

"Keep me posted. I know he's a good guy, and a good cop, but an ounce of prevention and all that." Lt. Ramos ruffled my hair as we left.

Antonio's was in the center of town, right on the waterfront with this great outdoor patio so you could hear the waves while you ate. The hostess took one look at Dad and Mr. Snuffles, who were both still in uniform, and seated us out there at a good distance from anyone else. I thought that might kind of defeat Mom's purpose, but the pretty sunset over the water helped me not to worry as much.

The serious talk didn't start until the food got there, which made me almost not want to eat. If they didn't want to be interrupted by the waitstaff, it must be pretty explosive. Still, the prospect of calamari cut through my fear.

"All right." Dad took a mouthful of ravioli and put his fork down. "Mallory, you have to realize why what you did was dangerous. You could have been seriously hurt or even—" He stopped, eyes bulging with the weight of a word he couldn't say.

I felt kind of bad for him. His whole job was dealing with terrible things happening to people. I was his only child, and he must have had all kinds of awful images going through his head. "Dad, I know you're worried about me. It's natural. It's normal. But those guys? They're not my fault. They came for us. All I was trying to do was stall until an adult could come and help."

"Really? So you didn't hit him with your hockey stick?" He sucked in his cheeks.

"Well, I wasn't going to let him touch me. Or the twins." I sat up a little straighter.

"If you hadn't gone digging out by the beach, you wouldn't be in this position in the first place." Dad glowered at Mom. "Which is why I'm especially disappointed in you, Liliana."

"Way to victim blame." Mom sipped from her glass of wine. "Do you go telling Sarah McCrory or Alan Scott not to let their kids go to the beach, and if they do, then it's their kids' fault if drug dealers go targeting them? Hm?"

"It's different." Dad sighed. "Their fathers aren't cops."

"So children of cops should expect to live under a perpetual lockdown, and anything that happens to them is their fault? That's absurd. It's ridiculous, and you know it. You told her to stay out of the woods, and she stayed out of the woods." It wasn't quite true, and Mom and I both knew it. I wasn't about to let facts get in the way of a good takedown of my dad though.

"So she goes out and interferes with drug dealers? Lil, I deal with this kind of people all the time. It's my whole job. These are not good people. They'll kill you without a second thought. You can't go letting her get mixed up with this stuff. It's—it's beyond stupid; it's negligent."

Something dangerous flared in Mom's eyes. "Mmm. So let me get this straight. The case in question was a theft from the museum, of a treasure that most certainly did not exist in the museum. She and her friends found a clue in that case when *you* didn't pick them up as agreed, leaving them stranded and forcing them to walk back to your house unaccompanied.

"They found a clue in a completely unrelated case while under adult supervision, did the actual right thing and contacted authorities instead of pocketing the cash, defended themselves from an attack until the numerous adults on the scene could intervene, but somehow, *I'm* negligent? I'm looking forward to discussing this with our attorneys and a judge, personally."

Dad gripped his fork so hard he bent it, but he didn't raise his voice. "Lil, you might write a good detective story, but you have no idea what it's like to actually deal with these people."

"Have you forgotten what I used to do before my books started selling?" Mom stared at him, impassive. "I know you never did like to discuss it. Mallory is a victim, along with the other kids. Do I *like* the fact that she was apparently targeted by a bunch of drug dealers? No. Am I comfortable with it? Also no. Am I concerned for her safety? Absolutely.

"Am I going to sit here and let you browbeat her into some kind of ridiculous notion that she's somehow to blame for any of this? Absolutely the heck not." She took a deep breath and sipped from her wine.

"Fred, I know you're scared."

Dad flushed scarlet. "I'm not scared—"

Mom held a hand up. "Don't give me that nonsense, I've known you too long. And I know every one of those men you work with, and I know your family. It's hard for you to express your fear. It's hard for you to express your love, which is one of the reasons we're not married anymore."

"That's not why we're here." Dad snapped the words out like a whip, but Mom was supremely unbothered.

"It's exactly why we're here, Fred. I know how much you love Mallory. I remember how happy you were when she was born, how much you loved holding her and carrying her around. I remember how much you loved bringing her to the station and showing her off. I remember how proud you were when she got interested in hockey, and how much you cheered when she scored her first goal."

Dad squirmed and glanced over at me.

I couldn't remember any of that. I couldn't hear anything but a general noise when I scored my first goal, and all that other stuff happened when I was just a baby. I tried to imagine my dad showing me off, and the image couldn't form.

"It's fine to be worried about what's happening. I'm terrified, personally. But it's not okay to take it out on

Mallory. She did nothing wrong here. What we can do is help to keep her safe. We can teach her to stay safer, we can help her to make good decisions going forward. But I'm not going to have you putting thoughts in her head that she can't come to us when she's in danger because it's just going to make you angry."

Dad closed his eyes and breathed deeply for a few moments. I could see him run his tongue over his teeth. He got some of his color back. "Okay. Fine. You might have some points there." He glared at her. "The digs about our marriage were uncalled for."

I stuffed my mouth with more calamari. Mom and Dad had split when I was maybe two. I couldn't remember a time when they'd been together, so I'd appreciated the history lesson.

Mom shrugged. "I felt it was necessary. It shows a pattern. It's not a criticism, necessarily. It's just an observation." She sighed and lost a little of her stiffness. "Everyone has their strengths, and things they're less strong with. That . . . challenge, I suppose . . . is probably an asset on the job."

Dad cleared his throat and turned his attention back to his dinner. Mom looked out over the water for a moment, and then her impassivity returned.

"So. Let's talk about how we can keep Mallory safest going forward."

I stifled a groan. I would have loved to hear more about their marriage, but it wasn't going to happen. Instead, they tossed ideas about restrictions and evasive moves around like a volleyball. I vetoed a couple, like quitting hockey camp. That was just too far. I was okay with not going back to the beach though, and I was definitely okay with not going anywhere alone.

"Look." I looked my dad in the eye. "I don't want anything to do with drug dealers, or drugs, or anything like that. It was cool to find the gems and everything. It was fun. Would it be cool to find the actual pirate treasure? Yeah. It's fun to do the research and to think of places it could be." I swallowed hard.

"But there's been *lots* of people over the years looking for Shatswell's treasure. It's a fun project. A pirate who's been dead for three hundred years can't come back and hurt us. I'm not looking to get involved with drug dealers or whatever those guys are. They're mean and they smell bad. If you want to make them go away for a very long time, I'm okay with that."

Dad relaxed a little bit. "We're still looking to get an ID on those guys. It was a smart idea for you to get Mrs. McCrory to get pictures of them without them noticing. We have some images from security cameras at the rink too. Hopefully, something will turn up soon."

"There are cameras in the rink?" I hadn't known that. I wasn't sure how to feel about it.

"Yeah. Most places with cash registers have them now." Mom gave half a grin. "Anyplace that's vulnerable to robbery, really. And considering that the rink has a bar . . ."

"It does?" I frowned. "I've never seen it."

"It's not open before five. And it's not exactly in direct view of the kids. But there are plenty of adults who play hockey for fun too. Anyway, let's focus on keeping you safe and not on bars." Mom winked at me and turned back to Dad. "What about prints on the drug dealers' Tupperware?"

"Haven't come back from the crime lab yet, but

we're hoping to get something soon." He rubbed at his face. "The way those guys smelled, according to people who had contact with them, they're probably not staying anyplace with running water. Makes them harder to catch."

I shuddered. "But not impossible, right?"

He gave me a smile that was probably meant to be reassuring. It didn't reach his eyes. "No, sweetheart. Not impossible."

CHAPTER THIRTEEN

I felt a little bit better after our dinner. Mom definitely knew how to handle Dad. He gave me a hug before we went our separate ways that night, which he hadn't done since the whole thing with the bag of gems in the woods blew up. Mom texted Lt. Ramos when we got home to let him know things had gone well, which seemed kind of strange to me but whatever. Things were better in Cavanland, and that was what mattered.

I did notice a police car parked outside the rink when we pulled up the next day, and coaches and staff had a bit of a grimmer set to their faces. It didn't take a rocket scientist to figure out why.

Megan, the goalie from my girls' team, nudged me as we got our pads on. "That was some intense stuff, huh? With the cops coming and everything? You're probably used to it though."

I made a face at her. We were friends, so I didn't hit her, even though I kind of wanted to. "I'm around cops all the time. Not creeps who sit there and threaten me. Dad's kind of careful about that."

"I guess he would be. You know what though? It was kind of awesome the way you hit him. You made it look all innocent and stuff, but anyone on the team knew what you were really doing." She grinned and bumped shoulders with me again.

My face got hot, right up to my hairline. "I had to do something."

"Hey, I'm not about to complain. It was awesome. With any luck you'll have scared those guys right off, or the cops did." She met my eyes. "And that means they won't make you stink on the ice anymore. Any of you three."

I laughed and pulled my sweater over my head. "Yeah, we were all pretty bad. Having them here was really throwing me off."

"But you kicked their butts." She waggled her eyebrows at me, and we both stuck our helmets on our heads. It was time to go out there and skate.

I skated better than I had since this whole thing started, and I scored three goals in the scrimmage after our break. Mom took me home, and there were no weird people in the massive lobby. All in all, it was a good day.

The weather was kind of crappy, so I stayed inside and played video games online with Viv and Megan. The Scott twins were home with their grandmother, so we didn't have to do the "but you kids are such good friends" stuff adults had been insisting on since the earliest learn-to-skate programs. Mom hid out in her office, probably dreaming up inventive ways of killing off characters. It was kind of what made her money, after all.

Dad stopped by after his shift to drop off Mr. Snuffles, like usual. Mom let him come in for a drink, and he gave us an update on both cases. "We still haven't found much about the museum robbery. I'm not sure we will, to be honest." He ran a hand through his auburn hair and glanced toward the window. "Whoever did it, and whatever it is that they took, is probably long gone by now."

I pretended to be deeply interested in my phone, so I wouldn't say anything. Dad and I had barely achieved peace yesterday with the whole museum thing. I didn't want to risk anything. Still, I had to wonder how there could be no trace of what had been taken. Was the museum not cooperating? And if not, why?

"What about the drug dealers?" Mom sounded calm, but she held herself perfectly still. She didn't even touch her wine, which is how I knew it was serious.

"They're in the wind too. Farley tracked them to the old power plant, and the trail goes cold there. We found a spot of antifreeze there, so they're driving some kind of vehicle with a slight leak. It's just like I thought yesterday— they're on the move, sleeping in their vehicle." He gripped his beer harder. I almost thought it would break.

"There's something they want here though." I had to speak up, just to stop Dad from breaking the bottle. "They won't go far."

I'd meant to give Dad some encouragement, but instead, the words hung in the air like a jail sentence.

"Thanks for the reminder, kiddo." His smile looked forced. "The good news is, I never meet the smart criminals. These guys thought it would be a great idea to attack kids at pickup, at youth hockey camp. I'm not sure how they managed to not know that was going to backfire on them, but it doesn't exactly say good things about their candlepower." He tapped his head. "They'll screw up soon, and they'll screw up too bad to get away. I just hope they do it before someone gets hurt."

It was like his words summoned the phone call. My phone jumped in my hands, ringing so loud it even made Mr. Snuffles jump.

I looked down at the screen. I'd known Noah had my number, but he'd never used it to call before—only to text. I almost ignored it. I was having a good conversation with my parents. They were treating me like a person, not like a little kid, and I didn't want it to stop. At the same time, both of the Scott brothers knew better than to call me for something stupid. No matter what our parents told us, we weren't friends.

"Noah?" I glanced over at my parents, who watched me with oddly intense looks on their faces. Well, Mom always looked kind of intense, but this was different. She knew Noah would never call me unless he had to.

"Mal? I'm at the pizza place. I'm in the bathroom."

"I so don't care. If you're having trouble, call the doctor."

"Mal! I'm being serious. It's that guy. The one with all the scars."

My heart almost stopped. "Did he see you?"

"Yeah. He grabbed me when I tried to go and get napkins. He said he was going to cut my throat from ear to ear." Noah sniffed. "He had a knife. No one else saw it."

I bit my lip and glanced at my dad. "Okay. You're at the one near your house, right?"

"Yeah. I'm locked in, but I can hear someone just outside the door. I need help."

"We'll be there right away." I hung up.

Dad and Mr. Snuffles were already on their feet. Mom had her keys in her hand. "Where are we going?"

"The pizza place." I ran out to the car with Dad

and Mr. Snuffles.

"There are ten pizza places within the town limits, Mallory." He gave me a dirty look.

"Only one near the Scott house. I think it's called Stavros'?" I took a deep breath and slid into the passenger seat of Dad's squad car.

"You can't ride in the front seat, you're only eleven!" He turned the key.

Mom was already pulling her car out of the driveway.

I buckled my seat belt. "The guy with the scars is there and threatened Noah with a knife."

Dad cursed and hit the lights. He didn't turn on the sirens, but that didn't bother me. I knew they didn't use the sirens when they didn't want to warn a suspect they were on their way. Dad had told me that before.

He radioed the dispatcher and explained the situation while he drove, weaving around traffic. I held on tight and tried not to picture my town team's best scorer with his throat cut. I could only breathe in short, shallow breaths.

We were only kids. Why would anyone want to cut our throats?

It didn't take long for us to get there, not the way my dad drove when he needed to get somewhere. Mom was right on his tail too, which kind of made me wonder what she used to do before I came along. We pulled into the no parking zone in front of Stavros' Pizzeria, which was a super casual place on the corner at the end of the street where the Scotts lived.

Dad snapped at me to stay in the car, but I ignored him and stayed with Mom. Dad and Mr. Snuffles, in the meantime, went into the pizza joint ready for action.

The restaurant was full of families in booths and at tables. A few minutes ago, they'd been happily eating. Now they stared in openmouthed terror as a cop and his dog went tearing into the back of the restaurant. The guys behind the counter shouted an obscenity as their workplace got invaded.

Mr. Scott figured out what was going on first. He turned to me and Mom as all color drained from his face. "Noah?"

Mom nodded as Logan jumped up and hid behind me.

"What do you think I'm going to do?" I glared at him.

The back of the restaurant, where the bathrooms were, was kind of hidden. There wasn't a lot of light, and stacks of chairs helped to screen the restroom doors from view. All I could do was hear Mr. Snuffles barking his head off.

Mr. Scott turned to my mom. "Why did he call you guys instead of . . . you know, us?"

"Everyone does strange things when they panic. When Fred gets him out of the bathroom, you'll get a chance to ask him." Mom gave him a little smile.

Other cop cars pulled up to the curb just as I heard something slam against wood. Someone else yelled, "Ow!"

Mr. Snuffles stopped barking.

Dad reappeared a few seconds later, frog-marching the scarred man from the rink toward the exit. Mr. Snuffles marched by his side. The scarred man had a red mark on his cheek, and his hands had been handcuffed behind him.

Mr. Scott fell back into his chair. It didn't look like

he was even seeing what was right in front of him.

I glanced around the pizzeria. I couldn't see any of the bad guys left, so I headed back toward the men's room. The door had some splintering near the handle, along with a big footprint.

I knocked on the door. "Noah? It's me, Mal."

"Is he gone?"

"He's gone. You're safe. Dad arrested him. You can come out now."

Nothing happened for a second, and then Noah opened the door. His eyes were red and puffy, and he sniffed loudly. I didn't say anything. Maybe I didn't like Noah, but I'd cry if I had to lock myself in a bathroom because someone was trying to kill me too.

"Cold water." I jerked my head toward the sink. "It helps."

He blinked at me for a second, and then he nodded. A few splashes from the sink helped make it less obvious that he'd cried, and we headed back out into the dining room.

Noah almost ran back to the bathroom when he saw my dad, but Dad put a hand on his shoulder. "I sent the guy back to the station with a couple of the other officers. It's okay. He's not getting out. You're still safe."

Logan walked up and hugged his twin. "I had no idea that was even happening. We thought you just had a bad reaction to the pizza. You know, with the cheese and everything."

Noah stuck his tongue out at Logan. "Shut up. No, I went to get the napkins like I said, but that guy grabbed me. He was hiding by the chairs, over where you can get into the bathrooms. He said he was going to cut my throat if I didn't give him the money we found."

"How did you get away?" Mom crouched down to his level, voice soft and about as threatening as a kitten. It was weird.

"I kicked him in the knee and ran into the bathroom. That's when I called Mallory. It was the first number in my contacts." He blushed. "Sorry. I panicked. I didn't know what else to do."

"It's fine." Dad grinned. "I mean 9-1-1 is probably better, but all things considered, it worked out okay. And Mallory would have called 9-1-1 for you if I hadn't been there. Obviously, you're going to have to come in and give an official statement."

Mr. Scott swallowed. "Yes, of course. We'll follow you."

Mr. Snuffles put his head on the table, clearly asking for a piece of the pizza. Noah gave him one. "He's obviously earned it."

CHAPTER FOURTEEN

It wasn't hard for me to put a brave face on things when we were at the pizza shop. I didn't even think about it, I just kind of did it. For one thing, Dad was on edge enough without having me freak out. He'd never say it out loud, but if he saw me acting the least bit scared, he'd have me locked down so fast I'd be lucky to see the light of day before I turned twenty-one.

For another, I'd heard Dad (and Mom, for that matter) talking about staying calm a thousand times. According to them, and pretty much anyone who'd ever worked as a first responder who I'd ever met, the absolute worst thing a person could do in an emergency was panic. It spread faster than stomach flu in a day care center. The people who showed up had to keep their marbles in one place, or a minor problem would turn into a major disaster.

Noah wasn't my friend. He was my teammate. He hadn't called the police or the fire department or even his dad. He'd called me. That made me a first responder, at least as much as the person who answered the phone when someone called 9-1-1. I had just as much of a role to play in staying calm as Dad or Mom.

And finally, there was no way I was going to let

Noah and Logan Scott see me freaking out, about anything, ever. Not in this lifetime.

At home though? In the safety of Mom's ancient house, built by my actual ancestors with loving hands to keep me safe?

I crawled into Mom's bed as soon as I could. My room was built of awesome and win, don't get me wrong, but it also kind of smelled like hockey and dog. Mom's room smelled like *mom*—lavender, maybe a little bit of sunscreen considering the time of year, and that shampoo she used. Her two cats kind of sniffed when Mr. Snuffles padded in with me, but the pets had made their peace with each other a while ago.

Mom put down her tablet and moved over, making room for me in the bed. She didn't ask why I needed to cuddle up. She didn't have to.

"So." She put the tablet on the bedside table. "That was exciting."

I got under the covers, and Mr. Snuffles hopped up onto the end of the bed. The cats scooted up and curled up onto Mom's other side, glaring daggers at my dog.

"It was scary." I swallowed. "I figured seeing the police come to the rink would be enough to make them go away."

Mom looked away for a second, and then she put her arm around me. "Honestly? I thought it would be too. I'm not sure why . . ." She trailed off. "Maybe this one just figured he'd try again. You know, independently."

The corners of Mom's mouth were tight though.

"There's something you're not telling me." I rested my head on her shoulder.

"There's a lot I don't tell you, sweetheart." She

kissed the top of my head. "It's a parent's job to tell their child anything the child can handle, and keep back what they don't think the child can't handle. You don't need to know about my wild and crazy life in undergrad, for example."

"How wild and crazy did it get?"

"There's a statute of limitations, and it's expired on everything." She winked at me.

I considered what I *did* know. "What did you used to do? Before I was born, I mean?"

She sighed. "I was a lawyer."

"Like Auntie Clara?"

"Er. Auntie Clara works in private practice. I was an assistant district attorney." I must have looked pretty blank because she clarified. "I was a prosecutor."

"So you know a lot of this stuff because . . ."

"Because it was my whole life for ten years before my life changed for the better." She gave me a little squeeze. "It didn't pay great, and I was already writing in my spare time. My books were taking off. Day care was expensive, and it would have taken up almost all of my salary, *and* I'd have had to give up writing. So." She shrugged. "I make six times what I made at the DA's office, and I'm able to be home with you."

I digested this for a minute. "How come Dad didn't quit his job and stay with me?"

"He didn't have the second job writing." She laughed. "It was my choice, love. But, yes, that's how I have the inside knowledge. It's also how I met your dad."

"Gross." I gave a full-body shudder at the thought. Sure, my parents must have dated at some point, but that didn't mean I wanted to know anything about it. "So you probably know a lot about guys like Scarface."

She hesitated, just long enough for me to realize she was choosing her words carefully. *She doesn't want me to freak out. Which means there's something for me to freak out about.*

"Well, every case was its own special little brand of fun." She snorted at some kind of memory I couldn't touch. "I'll admit to being concerned. In my experience, bad guys like—Scarface, was it?" She chuckled. "Like these fragrant friends don't last long in their business by being stupid. For all that we can make jokes about crooks tripping over themselves and making it easy, drug dealers who make stupid mistakes will either not be trusted or will get themselves killed."

I flinched. "Just for screwing up?"

She sighed. "With the amounts of money involved with the drug trade, and the potential penalties involved? Yeah. Scarface and friends aren't the big guns, but they report to other people. And those people aren't going to make themselves vulnerable.

"And maybe they can get away with going after kids whose families don't have these advantages, who can't be right there with their kids all the time. It shouldn't be that way, I want to see that changed, but right now, we have to work with what we're given. Guys at this level should know better than to go after kids whose families are right there in the rink, ready to step in and do something. Not only do they complicate things in the short term, but they have the time and energy to keep making a stink and harassing the authorities until the town gets too hot for the crooks to stay in."

I gripped the sheets. "Maybe these guys didn't have

anyone like that in their lives, so they can't think like that."

"It's an eighty percent chance you're right, and they didn't have that kind of privilege. Don't think for a minute it's not a privilege. At the same time, they *all* know the difference between kids who won't be reported missing or hurt and kids who will. Not that poorer parents don't love their kids, but reports don't get taken as seriously." She shrugged, but shadows appeared behind her eyes.

Her books always ended with the bad guys going to jail. I could only guess how many times they hadn't, back when she'd been a lawyer.

I took a deep breath. "Okay. So they did something stupid. Does that mean they're stupid or desperate?"

Mom grinned, and her eyes gleamed. "Asking the right questions. You're such a smart kid, Mallory. Since they wouldn't be in a position to handle money like you found by the Old Light if they were stupid, my guess would be desperate."

For a minute, I basked in Mom's pride. Then I remembered why I was in here wallowing in her bed instead of in my own. "Desperate isn't good."

"No." Mom took a deep breath. "It's actually pretty bad. Desperate people do stupid things. If they had any other choice, they wouldn't have come after kids in daylight, in full view of the whole league and their parents. And they wouldn't have gone after Noah in a crowded pizzeria."

I sank down so only my head was above the covers. The blankets wouldn't protect me, it was silly, but I felt better anyway. "So they'll come for us again."

Mom moistened her lips. "If this kind of police presence hasn't scared them off yet, then it's a safe bet that they'll keep coming. Yeah." She bowed her head. "I wish I could tell you something better. I wish I could say they're just going to go running back off to Portland or Boston or Providence or whatever dump they crawled out of, but this is twice they've come at children in a public place. They *can't* leave until they get the money."

I had to fight with this for a second. Nothing was worth going to jail for, was it? And definitely nothing was worth going after a cop's kid for. "But we can't give them anything! They have to know we turned it all in."

"It wouldn't be the first time criminals forced a child to do something for them. I've seen it before." She picked her head up. "Your dad, and the police here in Black Sail Bay, are doing everything they can to keep you and the others safe. They're pulling overtime to keep an eye on everyone's house—"

"How do you know that?" I rolled over to face her. "You don't work for them. And they've been dealing with budget cuts—"

She stroked my hair. It should have made me feel like a dog, but instead I felt calmer. Not calm, but calmer. "Lt. Ramos texted me."

"Does he text you a lot?" I wrinkled my nose.

"Only when it's important, honey. And when it comes to kids, it's *very* important."

Something was still eating at me, and I couldn't think of anyone else to ask. If I asked Dad, he'd tell me to leave it alone. If I asked Lt. Ramos, he'd say something nice, but he definitely wouldn't answer me. He probably couldn't.

"What does any of this—drug dealers, people going after children—have to do with the museum getting robbed or pirate treasure?"

Mom smirked. This wasn't the gentle smile of a comforting mother. This was the smirk of a coconspirator, or maybe the same look she got when she was plotting out one of her mystery books. "That's a pretty good question. There are a couple of possibilities here. What do you think they are?"

I tried not to roll my eyes. I failed, but Mom didn't mention it.

"So maybe they robbed the museum to draw attention away from what they were doing so no one would see them burying the drug money?" I sat up again, rubbing my hands together. "I mean that would be easy, right? All the police and everyone are all in the woods and focusing on the pirates and everything, and meanwhile, they're free to go do whatever down by the Old Light."

"Hm." She nodded a little. "That's an option. Of course, that creates an additional risk. If they're from out of town, they might not realize the museum doesn't have any decent security. They'd be risking getting their faces on camera—which would be stupid, and shorten their lifespan considerably."

Oh, yeah. Mom was definitely in murder-mystery mode now.

"So what else could there be?"

"Pure coincidence." She reached for her tablet. For a second, I thought the conversation was over, but she had something she wanted to show me. "Look, the museum says their admissions are up and they've received two hundred times as many donations for the month of July as they normally would."

I looked at the document she was showing me, but

it didn't make a whole lot of sense. "It's a board report?"

"Yep. Clara, Teresa, and I are all on the board. They're both coming over tomorrow to talk about it. But you see here how much better the financials are since the robbery. Better for this year than for all of last year, even though it's only half over."

"Okay, that's great, but what does it have to do with the drug dealers?"

"Nothing at all." She closed her tablet with a snort. "Which is part of the reason I've been texting with Lt. Ramos."

CHAPTER FIFTEEN

Dad came by the next night, after work. He usually did, but he generally dropped off Mr. Snuffles and took off again. This time, though, he stayed, and he brought the twins, Viv, and their parents with him.

Mom wasn't exactly enthusiastic about this change, considering that she hadn't been warned ahead of time. She muttered a lot of words I wasn't supposed to know, in English and in Spanish. I pretended not to notice.

Still, she managed to scrape together some cheese and crackers, and even found some fruit to set out with juice for us kids and wine or beer for the adults. "I'm guessing this isn't a social call." She wouldn't even look at Dad, and her smile to the other adults was tight.

"Mallory, why don't you take the kids into your room and show them some video game or something?" Dad glanced over at me.

Mrs. McCrory rolled her eyes. "Fred, come on. The kids are eleven, not six. They're the ones living this. They're old enough to be involved with this discussion."

I hugged her. The McCrorys were friends with both of my parents, so they never liked to get in between them. It meant she really believed what she was saying. She really believed in us.

Dad, on the other hand, grumbled from his seat. "Sarah, it's not that easy. They're children. They can't be expected to handle this."

"Well, no." Mom smiled blandly and swirled her wine in her glass. "That's what they have us for. Let's just get this over with so we can move forward."

I could hear Dad's teeth grinding, but at least he did what he needed to do. "Fine. So, we have a name on the charming soul who paid a visit to the pizza parlor yesterday."

Noah flinched, and Mr. Scott lost all the color in his face. "Is his name 'On My Way To Supermax' by any chance?"

Dad scoffed. "Unfortunately, no. He is at the Middleton House of Corrections at the moment, awaiting possible extradition to Rhode Island, New York, Pennsylvania, and New Jersey, in that order, in addition to the charges he faces for attacking you, Noah. Since all of his crimes were state crimes, there's no chance of him going to Supermax. And frankly, Attica should be unpleasant enough for him."

"So what is his name?" Logan spoke up from where he was trying to sneak a glass of wine. He wasn't a drinker—we were kids. He just wanted to see if he could get away with it.

He couldn't. Mom moved it away from him without acknowledging him and passed the glass to Mrs. McCrory, who hid a laugh behind her hand but accepted the drink.

Dad sighed. "His name is Toby Barrington. He's got a long list of criminal charges and convictions, running from simple assault to grand theft auto, possession of a class D drug with intent to distribute, use of a firearm in the commission of a crime, to other things we don't need to discuss right now. Mr. Barrington is seriously bad news."

I swallowed hard. Dad only started using the super formal cop language when he wanted to hide things, specifically hiding things he didn't want me to know about. "But he's not getting out. And he told you where to find the others, right?"

Dad looked down at his beer. "Well, he's going to be a guest of the Commonwealth until those other states get around to figuring out who gets him first. He's not going to get bail, that's for sure. But guys in an organization like that?" He toyed with the label on his bottle.

Mom cleared her throat a little. "It's safer for them to keep their mouths shut and not talk about what they know. If they talk, even if you offer them a lighter sentence, they won't live to see release day." She shrugged, but she stroked my hair to lessen the blow. "It's sad, and maybe it shouldn't be that way, but it is. He's not high enough up the food chain to qualify for witness protection."

Mr. Scott tilted his head a little. "How do you know that?"

"The name is familiar." She wrinkled her nose. "He used to run with a guy by the name of Marc Altman. That could be someone you look for."

Dad sighed. "You couldn't have told me that this morning?"

"You couldn't have told me the name this morning?" Mom didn't rise to Dad's bait. "It's not like he looks like he did fifteen years ago. None of us do. He's got a giant scar over half his face. Moving on, with those two names you and Lt. Ramos should be able to figure out who the other two are and what their habits are."

"This isn't one of your books, Lil." Dad glowered at her. "It's not that easy."

"It's not like she doesn't have experience here, Fred." Mr. McCrory cleared his throat. "This isn't about who's better at solving crimes. This is about our kids and keeping them safe. What are we going to do? I'm a little freaked out here. They came to the rink. They followed the Scotts to the pizzeria. What's next?"

Viv leaned over and whispered into my ear. "Are they always like this? Your parents, I mean?"

"You know they are." I inched away from the table.

"You'd think they'd get over it after all this time."

"Who knows why they do what they do? They're adults. It's, like, hormones or something."

"Ew." We both shuddered. "Maybe if we squirted them with a spray bottle, like kittens?"

"It could help."

The adults were still talking. "It's hard to say. I'd like to say they'd figure out they're not going to be able to get at these kids, but it doesn't look like they think they've got a choice." Dad rubbed at the back of his neck. "At this point, it seems like the best bet is to make sure no one goes anywhere alone. In an ideal world we'd put everyone—and I do mean everyone, parents, grandparents, and goldfish—into protective custody. We don't have the facilities to pull that off."

"The kids would find a way to sneak out onto the ice anyway." Mr. Scott chuckled, even if he hadn't recovered any of his color yet. "I wouldn't want them to. I'd forbid it. It would be the best way to make sure my boys

116

did it anyway, and if I know Mallory there's no way she'd let boys get more ice time than her."

I nodded. Mr. Scott apparently knew me pretty well.

"See, that's the problem. These kids have no understanding of the danger here." Dad stood up so fast he almost knocked his chair over. "I can tell them these guys are dangerous until I'm blue in the face, and they're still going to go out looking for some kind of pirate treasure."

I stood up. "These guys have nothing to do with pirate treasure, and you know it."

Mom pinched the bridge of her nose. "Not now, Mal."

Dad turned on me. "See? This right here is what I'm talking about. I've already grounded you once, and that was before we got drug dealers into the mix."

Viv bit her lip, but she stood up next to me. "I mean—I don't know where they came from, or anything about drug dealers really, but it sounds to me like the drug dealers were involved probably before the museum robbery. It's not our fault—and definitely not Mal's fault—that we ran into them while we were digging."

"If you'd done what you were told you wouldn't have come across them at all." Dad shook his finger at me.

"Not how it works." I stomped my foot, which was probably kind of childish, but it is what it is. "If you put me in a bubble, somewhere in an isolation chamber where I can't reach out to anyone or see the sunshine, some drug dealer can still find me if they want."

"Not helping." Mom looked up at the ceiling.

Noah winced, but he stood up next to me. "I hate to go against you, sir, because you did save me from that guy yesterday. But Mal's right. You can't just lock kids up and try to keep us from exploring the world, and think that's going to make us safer somehow. Things still happen."

Logan stood up. "Everyone else is standing up too."

"Look." Mrs. McCrory held her hands up. "Mr. Cavan already said he's not going to put everyone into protective custody, so let's everyone calm down. I think it is reasonable to say we have to be with someone at all times, because that's a reasonable precaution to take. It's okay for us to take reasonable precautions. You kids don't want us to just abandon you to the creeps, do you?"

We all shook our heads, hard. I didn't want to go anywhere without my mom. If I could get away with bringing an army of adults with me pretty much everywhere, I'd do it.

"I still think we should be doing more." Dad sat back down. "I'm not a hundred percent sure. The rink is as secure as it can be right now. We've got cops on-site during the hours when the kids will be there, and we've got extra patrols in all of our neighborhoods. We have the entire force looking for these jerks, along with the state police."

"If the state troopers are involved, they'll find the rest of them soon enough." Mom held up a hand. I guess she must have seen something in Dad's face. "Not because Black Sail Bay doesn't have a competent police force, but because you guys don't have the resources for this kind of trouble. They do. Our tax dollars pay for it; we might as well get some benefit for it."

Dad glared, but he also deflated a little. I'd count it as a win, even if Mom didn't. "All right. Well, I'm going to pass on that little tidbit you gave me to Lt. Ramos." He

118

made a show of pulling his phone out, and I guessed the conference was over.

I brought Viv and the twins into my room. I just wanted to get away, and I figured they did too. I wasn't wrong.

As soon as the door was closed, the twins flopped down on the bed in identical heaps. "Wow, that was intense." Noah covered his own face with a pillow. "Wake me when it's over, will you?"

I supposed I could be kind of sympathetic. After all, he was the one who'd been attacked. "I didn't really think it could be that bad." I squirmed a little. "Not until yesterday, anyway. Hopefully, what Mom told Dad means they'll find them fast."

"You don't really think that." Logan sat back up. "There's no way they're going to be able to figure out who the other guys are just from a case your mom half remembers from fifteen years ago. That's before any of us were even born. And if they don't feel like they have a choice other than trying to get us to get the money back for them . . ."

"Then they're stupid." Viv stuck her chin out. "Everyone knows once something goes into evidence it's locked up tight."

"They're probably counting on being able to threaten us into risking it. We're kids, and we don't have records. The courts would be easier on us." I sat down on my beanbag chair, which was probably made up mostly of dog hair at this point. "I'm worried."

"I didn't think you were scared of anything." Noah peered out from under the pillow.

"I'm not," I lied. "I'm *worried.* It's not the same

thing. Anyone with two brain cells would be worried. The fact is, the adults are worried too. They're trying to make a plan."

Noah scoffed and went back to hiding. "Your parents are the only ones who know what they're doing, and they're too busy bickering to come up with any real ideas."

I couldn't argue, even though I wanted to. "Yeah, well, that doesn't stop us from coming up with plans of our own."

CHAPTER SIXTEEN

Coming up with plans of our own sounded fantastic, but by the time our parents took off, we'd come up with about as many as they had. Maybe they had the advantage of being able to access police records and whatever, thanks to Dad, but we had the advantage of not needing to stop and argue about dumb stuff every ten minutes.

Okay, we had the twins, who had to stop and fight about chores, which one their dad liked better, whether or not their dad could tell them apart, and which one had stinkier farts. So maybe we didn't have such an advantage after all.

Either way, the only plan we were able to come up with by the time the sun went down was "hit them where they can't block and kick them while they're down." Sure, it sounds like dirty play, and I guess it kind of is. It was the strategy we used on my club team, where we regularly went up against high school teams twice our size. You do what you have to do.

I helped Mom clean up afterward because I knew she'd still be mad about Dad inviting people over to her house without her consent. She didn't need the extra aggravation. We did the work we had to do and then we made a light salad for dinner.

"After all that cheese and crackers, I don't need much." She grimaced and glanced at me. "Then again, I'm not playing hockey all summer. If you want, I can fix you something more substantial."

I shook my head. "We've got those rice things from the bulk store if I need it. I had a lot of cheese and crackers myself."

To be honest, I didn't feel much like eating. The drug dealers had me scared, and I wasn't ashamed to admit it either. If I admitted it was affecting me this badly, so I couldn't eat, I knew Mom would pull the plug on hockey and might even drag me back to Spain with her.

I wanted nothing in the world so badly as to go to Spain with my mom, but not because I was running off like a chicken. I wasn't going to abandon my friend and my teammates. Not like that.

So I made myself eat the salad, and we watched something fun on TV. I don't even remember what it was, just that it was mindless and kind of funny. Later on, I went to bed.

I expected to go to bed and sleep straight through until morning because I'm a normal person and that's kind of what normal people do. It's what they do under normal circumstances, anyway. These weren't normal circumstances, so I guess I shouldn't have expected a normal sleep cycle.

Mr. Snuffles started growling at three in the morning. I jerked awake, my heart racing. Mr. Snuffles didn't growl. Maybe he did when he was on the job, but when the vest was off, he was basically a teddy bear with bad breath.

I turned the light on. Everything looked pretty much normal.

Just then, someone started slamming on the door, while someone else rang the doorbell about a thousand times. If anyone asks, tell them I bravely jumped up and grabbed a spare hockey stick I keep under the bed for times like this.

The truth is, I hid under the covers.

Mr. Snuffles had no interest in hiding in the bedroom. He headed right for my bedroom door, barking like it was his job.

I pulled myself together. I wasn't alone in the house. If Mom was in danger, I couldn't just let the drug dealers or evil clowns or whoever take her. I had to do what I could to save her. I jumped out of bed, took my hockey stick in shaking hands, and opened the door.

Mr. Snuffles ran out into the hall and down the stairs. Mom, being Mom, was already at the door. She must have peeked out, because she was opening it up as I spoke.

Mr. Snuffles stopped barking and sat down, tongue lolling out. As far as he was concerned, nothing was wrong.

Viv and her mom were at the door, still in their pajamas. Viv was clutching her favorite stuffed animal, a rainbow-colored llama she called Alexander, so tight I thought she might break it. She looked white as a sheet under all her freckles, and Mrs. McCrory didn't look any better.

"Sarah! Vivianne!" Mom ushered them in and locked the door behind them. "Oh my God, what's wrong?" She turned lights on as she spoke. "Mal, get a glass of wine for Mrs. McCrory. You can make a hot cocoa for you and Vivianne after that."

I rushed to obey. Viv stayed right by my side, so close I could feel the way she was shaking. I poured a glass of wine for Mrs. McCrory, made some hot cocoa for Viv, and brought her back to my room. "I'm guessing you guys are staying here tonight."

Viv nodded. "If your mom lets us, that is."

"She's not going to kick you guys out. I can see you two are terrified. You're basically family. She'd never send you out to deal with whatever made you feel this way." I patted the bed. I didn't have a bunk bed or anything, but my bed here was big enough for both of us. We could share.

She climbed in and took a sip of her cocoa. "One of the guys showed up at the house. The—" She cut herself off, squeezing her eyes shut. "The drug dealers."

I stifled a scream with my hand. "Are you sure?"

She nodded, looking down. "I saw him. It was the one with the weird mustache. He broke the window. He was trying to break in." She took a deep, shuddering breath. "I'd gotten up to get a drink of water. And I heard breaking glass. I went downstairs to see what was wrong. Dad was right behind me."

I wrapped my arms around her. "Is that where your dad is? Fighting the burglar?"

She nodded. "I mean, he called 9-1-1. I hope he's not fighting the guy. But he told me and Mom to get in the car and go. We came here." She sniffed. "We didn't know where else to go."

Dad's house would have been a good bet because Dad had guns and stuff. But Mrs. McCrory wasn't as close with Dad as she was with Mom, so maybe she just wouldn't have thought of it. "You must have been so scared."

She looked up at me. "I still am scared, Mal. What

have we gotten ourselves into? We're just kids. We're not supposed to be dealing with drug dealers and people trying to break into our house. We're supposed to be going to the beach, having fun, going to school, and pushing back against our parents just enough to make them dread our teenage years."

"You're not wrong. Except maybe about that whole beach thing. Sunburns are not my friend." I managed a wry grin. "The thing is, Viv, none of this is our fault."

"Isn't it? We're the ones who decided to go poking around, looking for the stupid pirate treasure. Your dad told us it was stupid, but we did it anyway, and now these three drug dealers are trying to kill us."

I counted to five. She sounded like my dad, and I wasn't up to dealing with my dad right now. At the same time, Viv had been my best friend since the two-year-old room at preschool. I didn't want to drive some kind of wedge between us. "Look, like you said, we're kids. Looking for pirate treasure is perfectly normal for kids. We are not responsible for other people's choices. We were in the wrong place at the wrong time."

"But—"

"Viv, if this was your favorite YouTuber, would you still be blaming her for it?"

"Well, no, of course not." She bit her lip. "But it's different for us."

"Really isn't." I leaned back against the pillows. "Mom says we should be as kind to ourselves as we are to strangers. It makes sense, you know? It doesn't make sense to sit here and say, 'Oh, you should have planned for a bunch of crooks to do something bad, that doesn't even make sense for crooks.'"

She giggled a little at that. "Okay, maybe not. I still feel like there has to be something we could have done to avoid all of this."

"Sure. We could have all been born someplace else. Like, uh . . ." I wracked my brains. "Quebec. Yeah, Quebec. If we lived there, everyone would be thinking about hockey, not drugs, and we'd all be eating poutine."

She laughed out loud this time. "Mal, there's crime everywhere, and poutine is gross."

"Is not!"

"Your mom called it 'an abomination in the face of the taste buds!' "

"Even my mom can be wrong about a few things." I stuck my tongue out. "Come on—if I'm going to be the first female forward for the Bruins I have to be able to eat proper Canadian food."

She laughed so hard she kicked her feet, earning us both unamused glowers from Mr. Snuffles. "Mal, the Bruins are a Boston team. Boston's not in Canada!"

"They are for hockey purposes!" I was just teasing her, and it worked.

She soon drained the rest of her hot cocoa, and we were able to turn off the lights and go to sleep.

Mom and Mrs. McCrory came to camp with us the next day, and stayed in the bleachers the whole time. Apparently, Mom hadn't gotten Mrs. McCrory to laugh about hockey or poutine, because she looked like she'd just marathoned fifteen horror movies at once. She did tell Viv that the police had come for her dad, and he'd spent the night with my dad.

Dad met us after camp and made us all come down to the station, because of course he did.

"Still think this is a game?" he asked me.

Lt. Ramos got between us. "Fred, go walk it off." He put his hand on Dad's shoulder. "I know you're worried. Don't take it out on your family."

Dad glared at his superior, but he followed his orders. Mr. Snuffles nuzzled my hand before following Dad out the door.

Lt. Ramos took me and Viv into one of the interrogation rooms. It was a tiny smelly room, and we both kind of balked when we walked into it. "You'll have to forgive the room. We don't exactly have a ton of space available, if you know what I mean. I need to get a statement from you, Vivianne. And I figured that Mallory wouldn't be willing to be apart from you right now."

"More like the other way around." Viv laughed nervously. "You know she came down to the door with a hockey stick, right?"

Lt. Ramos shook his head. "Call 9-1-1, Mallory. Don't go in and fight these guys yourself, do you understand? They're dangerous. I get that when you're in the middle of things it can feel like you don't have a choice, and sometimes you really don't. But calling 9-1-1 first can still mean the cavalry's on its way, and the difference between life and death. Okay?"

I nodded. He was right.

Viv told Lt. Ramos pretty much what she'd told me. He asked some questions I hadn't thought to ask, which made me feel pretty stupid until I remembered it was his actual job to know to ask those things. "The mustache pretty much narrows down his identity to a couple of people." He pulled out a binder with a bunch of photos. "Do you see the man who tried to invade your house in here?"

Mallory didn't hesitate. She pointed to one man near the middle of the selection. "This one, sir."

He turned to me. "Mallory, does this man look familiar to you?"

I looked at the face Mallory had chosen. "He didn't speak, but he was definitely one of the guys at the beach and at the rink. He should be on the tape from the registers, right?"

Lt. Ramos winked at me. "Right as rain, Mallory. The good news is, we know who he is. That'll help us figure out where to find him. In the meantime, we're going to want you girls to be extra safe, okay? You're going to keep staying with Ms. Corwin and Mallory. I'll send a couple of guys to go pick up your things with you, just in case."

I glanced at Viv. On the one hand, I loved the idea of an extended slumber party with my best friend. On the other, this didn't exactly sound like something to celebrate.

CHAPTER SEVENTEEN

The next day, we all went to hockey—every last one of us. I felt kind of bad for Viv. She'd come for scrimmages when Mom was in Spain, but she hadn't had to stay for the whole day before. She seemed to be doing okay; she had her tablet and the rink had Wi-Fi, but I still felt bad. I knew she'd rather have her pool and the sunshine.

I refused to feel guilty. It wasn't my fault. It was the drug dealers. They'd made the choices, not me.

Somehow, that thought didn't exactly fill me with joy either.

After hockey, we went back to my place. Mom was going to get her time with her sisters tonight, and we were going to have a nice dinner at home. I'll admit I was excited about it. I hadn't seen my aunts in almost two months, and they were two of my favorite people in the world. Plus, eating at home meant I'd get to cook with Mom.

Mom can be kind of twitchy in the kitchen. Her mom didn't teach her to cook. She learned in Spain, with her grandmother, who didn't like to let other people into the kitchen either. It's hard for Mom to be patient and everything, but she tries because she knows how badly I want to learn. I think she's also secretly afraid I'll learn to cook from my Nan and cover everything in "white sauce" too.

So I cherished this chance to help Mom cook some of the food we both loved. Most of the dishes she was making were vegetarian because apparently Auntie Teresa was in "one of her vegetarian phases," but that didn't bother me at all. I hate cooking with meat. It feels gross, even if I like how it tastes. We still had a couple of dishes with meat or fish, but not a lot.

I know it sounds like a lot of food, and it is. Mom only knows how to cook for an army. Any leftovers meant we wouldn't have to cook for a while, so it all worked out well in the end.

Viv hadn't had to cook with Mom before, so she was a little intimidated by the whole thing. We chopped a ton of garlic, and don't even get me started on the vegetables. It was a ton of work, but it was worth it. Mrs. McCrory pitched in too, so everything got done in half the time it would normally take.

Aunt Clara showed up first, which kind of surprised me. She's a lawyer, but she does a lot of family law and lawsuits and stuff. She works a lot of long hours, and if she'd just been in Spain for however long she'd be struggling to catch up. Apparently, she hadn't gone back to the office yet though.

She hugged my mom and me, and Viv and Mrs. McCrory too. "It's so good to see you all! How are you? I've heard about all the drama. It must be terrible for you."

Mrs. McCrory blushed. "It could be worse. Liliana has been kind enough to let us stay here. The girls are already like sisters, so they have that going for them."

Clara took a picture of me and Viv with her phone.

"I'm sure you two are making the very best of it," she said to us with a little wink. "Mallory, would you bring me a glass of wine? I've been trying to unpack all day."

Viv and I brought out wine for everyone. I brought out a glass for Aunt Teresa too because I knew it wouldn't take her long to show up, and I was right. She showed up five minutes after we delivered the grown-ups' wine, and much to my mother's annoyance, it was my dad who dropped her off.

Teresa shook him off as soon as she crossed the threshold and gave him a look that should have killed him on the spot, muttering something in Spanish that I should have understood but didn't, and stomped over to the couch. She looked a little more put together than she usually bothered with, possibly because of her recent return from Spain. Her outfit only had one stain on it, a brownish-red one that I really hoped was only rust or something.

Dad saw me looking. "It's rust, from when we caught her trying to break into the station."

"It's just like you to try to hide the real situation, Freddie." She took off the ball cap she'd been wearing.

Viv leaned over to me and whispered into my ear. "Is that hat . . . lined with tinfoil?"

I just nodded. Aunt Teresa's oddities almost never surprised me anymore. I forgot that other people weren't used to them.

"First of all, Terri, there's this great thing called the Freedom of Information Act. Look it up. Second, do you think there might be a reason we might keep certain details quiet? Like your niece's safety, maybe?"

"No one in their right mind trusts cops with

anyone's safety." Teresa fixed my dad with another dirty look. "Even the best of you are mind-controlled by the Illuminati. And you're not the best of them."

Mr. Snuffles let out a whine, lay down, and covered his ears with his paws.

Mom gave a brittle little smile. "Well, we're not here to stress out about the Illuminati, chemtrails, the New World Order, or fluoridation right now. We're here to reconnect and unwind. What was her bail, Fred?"

"She covered it herself." Dad rolled his eyes. "Who knew that conspiracy theory coverage was such a growth industry?"

"Maybe if you pigs were more up-front—"

Mom shut Teresa up with one look. "Eat your bread, Teresa."

Dad closed the door behind him and grabbed an empty seat. "Mallory, why don't you go get me a beer?"

Clara sniffed. "You're not staying, are you?"

"Of course I'm staying. It's a family dinner. I'm Mallory's father. I have every right to be here." Dad smiled at her, that big fake smile he gave when he was messing with people.

I sighed and got him a beer. Viv followed me. So did Mr. Snuffles.

"He's not really going to stay, is he? I mean he wasn't invited." Viv frowned. "I don't mean to be rude about your dad. And maybe your mom did invite him."

"She didn't. Believe me. She doesn't want him around any more than my aunties do. But he thinks he needs to be here for some reason, and she doesn't want trouble." I found the beer in the fridge. "Mom keeps his beer around, you know? They usually get along much

132

better than this."

"I'll take your word for it." She glanced at the door to the living room. "What's with your aunt?"

"Teresa? She's just different, that's all. She likes to yank Dad's chain, and he's never liked my aunts to begin with." I snorted. "You know how it is."

"I never want to be an adult, if it's like that." She shuddered. "I'll just have cats and maybe be your manager when you play for the Bruins."

"Sounds good." We high-fived each other and then headed back into the other room.

"Look. It's this simple. Those dealers are still in the wind. It doesn't make sense to put the kids out in the open like that." Dad spread his hands wide. I put his beer in one of them, and he gripped it reflexively. "We're able to protect this house, but we can't keep sending cars to watch the camp for hours. It's not reasonable."

"The camp is a relatively safe space." Mom rolled her eyes. "They got in there once. I don't see it happening again, not with the way the other parents have been on edge about it. I get that there are budgetary constraints."

Viv and I exchanged glances. Were they seriously pulling police protection? The day after someone tried to break into Viv's house? She edged closer to me, and I put my arm around her shoulders. Mr. Snuffles moved to protect both of us.

"I find it fascinating that it's you coming here to talk about pulling the kids from hockey instead of Lt. Ramos, who is the senior officer assigned to the case." Clara looked bored as heck as she sipped from her wine, but she always did when she addressed Dad. It's part of why he hated her so much—well, that and the fact that she'd been

Mom's lawyer in the divorce.

"I'm being proactive, Clara. Nothing more exciting than that."

"Should we discuss this with him, I wonder?" She smirked. "Of course, if you wanted him involved with this discussion you'd have brought him. You didn't. Instead you chose to bring your former sister-in-law here, as though you were doing her a favor releasing her from prison."

"Hey, don't go putting weird motives onto me." Dad pointed at her.

I grabbed Viv, and we headed out into the backyard. I didn't need to be there for family fighting, and neither did she. We headed over to the little arbor, which had a bench underneath it where we could sit. "I just want this whole thing to be over." She leaned her head onto my shoulder. "Don't get me wrong, I love staying with you, but I want to stay with you because you're my best friend and we're having fun, you know? And I want you to come and stay with me too."

"Right?" I closed my eyes and took a deep breath of the salt air. "I honestly want to stop being scared. I've never been afraid of anything in my whole life."

"You're afraid of clowns, Mal."

"Anyone in their right mind is afraid of clowns. They're the creepiest things on earth. This is different. This is actual people who've done terrible things, out here looking to kill us. Or something. And my parents are being weird about it, which is making everyone else kind of weird about it. I just want everything to go back to normal." I kicked at the ground. "Summer should be for having fun, not for hiding and having my dad threatening to pull me out of my favorite thing to do. Not for hiding."

"Right?" Viv picked her head up. "I don't want to go back to school and have to say, 'Well, I hid in my best friend's bedroom' when people ask what I did with my summer vacation."

I slouched in my seat. "Ugh. School. Can you imagine? Want to bet they'll try to pull us out of school too?"

"Wouldn't that be better?" She scrunched up her nose.

"I don't know about you, but having my mom try to teach me science sounds like the absolute pits. She'll try to relate everything back to dead bodies because that's what she knows. And Dad wouldn't be any better. Math? Forget it. And neither of us would be able to get out of the house or see *anyone*. It would be just like lockdown but worse." I shook my head, red hair hitting me in the face. "Nope. Not doing it."

"So what are we going to do?"

I stood up. "Well, for one thing we're going in there to make my family stop bickering. And then we're going to figure out just how we can fix all this."

Viv stood up too. "I'm all for stopping the bickering, but how are we supposed to fix anything? We're kids. We can't do the kind of research your dad can—or your mom. If they choose to pull you out of hockey, or all of us from school or whatever, there is nothing we can do about it."

I nodded slowly because she was right. "Then we'll just have to make sure they make the right choices. Because I am not going to let them lock me up like some kind of princess in a tower."

CHAPTER EIGHTEEN

The next couple of days went pretty smoothly. I won't say they were normal because they weren't. The only place that was normal was the ice. We were all jumpy, even in the locker room, and to make things even worse Dad moved the Scott twins in with my mom and the rest of us.

He didn't warn her about that either. I'll let your imaginations do the work on how that turned out.

I did not like living with boys, even a little bit. Mom was able to make up some space for them all in the basement, which was at least finished and had a bathroom and stuff. That was good because I wasn't about to share my bathroom with two guys who think the height of humor is the existence of poop. At first, the twins balked at staying in the basement on the grounds that it had to be haunted.

Viv had a plan. "Well, that's just fine. Mal and I have been doing the sleepover thing every night. Tonight, we were going to paint each other's nails. Tomorrow we were going to watch some makeup tutorials and see if we can manage to copy them. And then the next night we were thinking of playing Light as a Feather—which will go so much better with more people, all things considered."

We gave them identical, sweet smiles that had all color draining from their faces.

"Er, the basement will be fine." Noah tugged at the collar of his T-shirt. It was already pretty stretched out, which meant he either spent a lot of time tugging on it or tried to put it on over his helmet. Either could be true.

"Yeah, no need to be mean about it." Logan shuddered.

"I've got some pretty silver nail polish." I spoke with some enthusiasm, trying to be convincing. "It will almost look like chrome in the right light. You can finally look like Wolverine!"

"Shut up." Logan's face turned scarlet, and he fled for the basement.

Noah cackled and high-fived me. Then he headed for the basement too.

Out on the ice though, everything else faded away. The only things that mattered were the puck, the goal, and the people trying to get between the first two. I was getting faster and better every day, and the better I got, the more likely it was that I'd become the first female forward to play for the Bruins.

The first guy, the one with the scar on his face, got extradited to Rhode Island to deal with an armed robbery conviction. I wasn't entirely sure why someone would have to get extradited from one part of the US to another, but Mom explained it was perfectly normal.

"It's a bit of a pain when it works against us, but it's not something you have to worry about right now. The important thing is he's going to stay behind bars, in a place that's much more secure than pretrial detention." She gave a little grin.

It turned out Mr. Scott was a decent cook, which I didn't expect. He took his turn cooking with Mom and Mrs. McCrory. He liked to grill, which was fun to watch, and I was never one to turn down a tasty cheeseburger.

None of us kids were allowed out much, but we tried to make the best of it. We got on each other's nerves a bit, but Mom had a big yard that gave us a lot of privacy and we were able to stay out of one another's way. At night, we could usually agree on something to watch while the grown-ups relieved their anxiety in another room. If Viv and I were unhappy about having the boys around, the boys were just as unhappy about having to be here.

"Why does your dad want to lock us up with you girls anyway?" Logan tossed a piece of popcorn at Mr. Snuffles, who caught it in his mouth and ate it. "It's stupid."

I bristled. Not that it wasn't stupid, because it was, but no one got to call my dad stupid but me. (And Mom, because no one was going to stop her.) "He's got his reasons."

"I'm sure he does, but he hasn't shared them with the rest of us." Noah glared at his twin and gave me this little, apologetic smile. "It's easier to do what you're told when you know why. It feels less crummy."

I sighed because as much as I wanted to argue with him on general principles, I knew he was right. "He doesn't tell me any more than he tells you." I rubbed at my temples. Living with boys was giving me a headache. "If he did, I'd pass it along."

"It feels kind of silly, doesn't it?" Viv tilted her head to the side. "The bad guys already know where I live, so our place is right out. And they found you at the pizza place, so they probably know where you live too."

Noah shrank back. His face had turned a little gray. "Yeah, let's not talk about that."

I perked up. I understood now. "It's the names. They figured out the names."

All three of my companions stared at me like I'd lost my mind. Only Mr. Snuffles trusted me to know what I was talking about. He rested his head in my lap while whatever mindless sitcom we were watching played out on the TV.

"Names?" Viv blinked at me. "You want to be a little more specific there?"

I took a deep breath. "They somehow figured out our names. I don't know how, but they did it. You can find the addresses on the internet—like, in the public records and stuff."

"The article." Noah hid his mouth with his hand, just for a second. "The article in the paper. The one we were all so excited about."

"Exactly." I snapped my fingers and ignored the sick feeling in the pit of my stomach. "That's how they were able to figure out who we were. But right now, and until we go back to school, I live with my mom."

"And your mom doesn't have your last name." Viv grinned. "She kept her own last name."

"So it's harder for them to find us here." Logan nodded slowly. "Okay, I get it now. I still think it stinks, but it's better than just him making us live here because he wants to get back together with your mom."

I cringed. "Trust me. He doesn't want to get back together with my mom. And there's no way she'd get back together with him. Let's stop thinking about my parents dating, please. Ever."

All of us could agree on that. We went about our business and headed for bed, expecting the next day to be more of the same.

Dad didn't show up to pick up Mr. Snuffles the next day. Mom waited as long as she possibly could, and then she called Dad as we were pulling out to go to the rink. She didn't get an answer.

This made me nervous, but I didn't say anything. I could see it made her nervous too, and I didn't need to add to it. Sometimes, when two people are both anxious about something they can feed each other's fear, and make it into something big and terrifying. I didn't want that to happen here, so I kept my mouth shut.

Mom was probably thinking the same thing. She's the one who taught me that, after all.

Lt. Ramos showed up right around the time the scrimmage was supposed to start. He waved and gave me a big smile, so I didn't freak out as much as I would have otherwise. I liked Lt. Ramos, and I was pretty sure he liked me, but he didn't exactly show up to camp to watch me play. He looked cheerful enough though, so I went ahead and played my little heart out.

After camp let out, Mom and Lt. Ramos met up with us. Mr. Snuffles was still with her. Mom had a little bit of tightness around her eyes and a weird set to her jaw, but Lt. Ramos was all smiles. "Hey, kids. We're all going to head over to the station for a hot minute. Is that okay?"

We looked at each other and shrugged. It wasn't as if we had a choice, even if he was asking if it was okay.

When we got to the station, it wasn't hard to see why Dad hadn't been over to pick up Mr. Snuffles. Dad had a black eye and a cut on his lip. His left arm was in a cast.

I ran over to him. "Dad!" I threw my arms around him. "Dad, what happened?"

He hugged me close. "You should see the other guy, kiddo." He patted Mr. Snuffles with his good hand. "Speaking of which, I need you guys to come down to one of the interrogation rooms and take a look at someone for me. Think you can do that?"

Mom stepped forward. "Fred, I'm glad you're doing okay, but I'm not comfortable with you having these kids get into another confrontation with the stalkers."

Dad bristled. It was wild, you could see the hair on the back of his neck actually stand up. "I'm not an idiot, Lil."

Lt. Ramos put his hand on Mom's shoulder. "Lil, they'll be observing through the one-way mirror. They'll be safe."

Dad—who was still in his pajamas, which was weird to see among all these uniformed cops—led us down to the interrogation rooms. "Just take a look through this window and let us know if you recognize this guy."

We looked. There was a guy in there with two black eyes, a broken nose, what looked like a broken jaw, and his arm in a sling. I could still recognize him though. His tattoo was pretty distinctive. "I've seen him. He was one of the guys on the beach." I looked over at Dad. "Where did you find him?"

"My living room." He ground his teeth. "Let's head back up to the lobby."

We obeyed, but my mind was spinning. Why was one of the beach guys in my dad's house?

My stomach lurched as I remembered our conversation from the night before.

Dad sat down. Mom passed him a bottle of water. I have no idea where she found it or anything. Dad took a deep breath and looked around at all of us. "I woke up at around six when I heard glass breaking. I sent a text to dispatch so the intruders wouldn't know I was awake, and then I went downstairs to make an arrest.

"There were two of them. One of them got away. I've already given a description to Lt. Ramos, because yes, Liliana, I do know how to do my job. I told them they were under arrest. They declined to surrender." He caught my eyes. "If they'll do this to me—an armed police officer—think about what they'll do to you."

I looked away. My dad had fought two intruders, people who had broken into his house looking for something.

Looking for me.

It wasn't hard to figure out. They'd gone for the twins. They'd gone for Viv. Of course they'd come for me next. I could understand it in my head. Looking at what they'd done to my dad was something else entirely. "Are you okay?"

"He's going to be on desk duty for a little while." Lt. Ramos put his hand on my shoulder. "Your dad's a tough cookie, Mallory. It takes more than a couple of out-of-town jerks to get him down. But, obviously, you have to take this very seriously. Your dad is right—he's a trained police officer. You're good hockey players, all of you, but you're not a match for these kind of criminals."

I gulped, but Noah took up the speech for me. "Sir, we'd never go up against guys like that on purpose. Only long enough to get away. You have to know that."

"I know." Lt. Ramos gave a little smile. "It's just—we worry. It's kind of our job, right?"

Dad didn't join in the smile.

CHAPTER NINETEEN

This latest attack was scarier than any of the others so far. Someone had actually been hurt. The fact that the *someone* in question was my dad, and he'd apparently beaten the snot out of the person who'd attacked him (and arrested him to boot), didn't make much of a difference. It could have been any of us. The creeps hadn't gone in looking for trouble with a cop, they'd gone in looking for a kid.

I'm sure you've already figured out that Mom and Dad had another epic fight about pulling us out of hockey that night. They had their fight right there in front of us kids. The only reason the boys and I were still allowed to play hockey was because the McCrorys and Mr. Scott put their feet down.

"Look." Mr. Scott took the beer Dad offered him, but he also gave my dad a long hard stare that had even my dad moving backward a little. "I understand that the kids are in danger. I understand *we're* in danger. It's crossed my mind more than a couple of times."

"Good." Dad managed a little smile. "Then you'll understand why we have to lock these kids down tighter than Fort Knox."

I didn't know where Fort Knox was or why it was

locked down so tight. I just knew if I got locked down tighter than some famous fort with the Scott twins, I would probably burn down my own house to get away from them.

And that would cause all kinds of complications, starting with the loss of all my hockey equipment.

Mr. McCrory shook his head. "I don't have skin in the game when it comes to hockey, but I *am* a doctor. And as a doctor, I know what locking them up like that would do to them. For one thing, they'd wind up doing something stupid just to get a breath of fresh air."

"We're not stupid, Dad." Viv stood up from her chair, eyes blazing. "We didn't do anything to cause this. This all came because a bunch of jerks decided to do crimes and then decided to come after a bunch of kids when we found their stash."

Mr. McCrory put his arm around Viv's waist and pulled her close. "I didn't mean to imply there was anything wrong with you. You're kids, sweetheart. You're normal. And normal kids need to be out and about. You need to be around other kids; you need to get some kind of stimulation. Right now, the police don't have any good leads on where these creeps might be."

"We're working on that." Dad stiffened. "You have to let us do our jobs."

"Fred, no one's saying you're not doing your jobs." Mom rolled her eyes and grabbed for a piece of cheese from the large platter in the middle of the table. We'd been eating a lot of this stuff lately. It couldn't be healthy.

"Everyone here knows this is a complicated, challenging case." Mom fixed Dad with a murderous stare. "And that's about as much ego stroking as I'm inclined to do. Dave is just saying you can't sit there and act like children are little robots who obey mindlessly and just turn off when you flip a switch. Because they're not."

"It's not like I don't spend time with Mallory and her friends too, Lil." Dad's face turned red, where it wasn't purple with bruises.

"That's why I'm surprised you just don't get it." Mom curled her lip.

I grabbed my friends and ushered them out of the room. We didn't need to see any more of this. *I* didn't need to see any more of this.

We hid in my room, which was becoming a refuge any time Mom and Dad argued. Mr. Snuffles came with us because while he was obviously worried about my dad, he wasn't about to leave me undefended with all the tension in the house.

"It's a good thing your folks live apart." Noah threw himself into my beanbag. "Are they always like this?"

"They're always like this when we're here." Logan grabbed a puck off my bookshelf and tossed it into the air. "Maybe it's us."

"You guys would drive anyone to argue." Viv shrugged. "Mr. Cavan gets really tense when he thinks Mallory's safety is an issue. I'm sure your dad isn't always a ray of sunshine."

I bumped shoulders with her, silently showing my gratitude. "Seriously. We've got to find some way to make sure we can still at least get to hockey. I'm not going to let a bunch of drug dealers who can't figure out where the soap is stop me from playing for the Bruins."

"You do know the Bruins are a men's team." Logan curled his lip and looked me up and down. "Last time I heard you were still a girl."

"There's a first time for everything, Badger Boy. Mom's taller than their star winger right now, so it won't be my size that holds me back. And you've both played against me. You know it won't be my ability to take or give a hit." I cracked my knuckles. "I might never be big enough to be a blueliner, but I'm going to take my shot at left wing. And I'm going to be the best they've ever seen. These jerks don't get to take it away from me." I sat up straighter.

"And you know what? I've known both of you since learn-to-skate. Noah, you want to play center almost as much as I want to play left wing. You've got the speed. Do you seriously want to let these guys who came up from where the heck ever make you have to be an . . . an accountant? A chemist?

"Logan, I'll deny it if you ever tell anyone I said anything good about you, but you've got the best defensive skills of anyone on our town team. You know you want to play D just like we want to score. Do you want to get stuck selling insurance in Black Sail Bay forever?"

Logan gave a full-body shudder, but then he looked at me. "There's always next year."

I scoffed. "Sure. Next year. Except we'd be going up against kids who got to do the full camp this year, and let's be real—we're not going to get playing time in the fall if we quit halfway through summer camp. Assuming Dad's coworkers can even find the bad guys before the regular season starts. There's no guarantee."

Viv nodded. "An injury would be different. This . . . well, you're not hurt. We're just sitting here waiting. It's not as bad for me because I'm not into the whole sports thing so much, but for you?"

"Okay, but you saw your dad." Logan shook his

head hard. "And he's a cop, you know? He's used to fighting bad guys. I'm fine with fighting a couple of kids on the ice, but the people we're dealing with are something else. They'll kill you. When I think about it that way, selling insurance doesn't look that bad."

Noah gazed at his twin with his nose wrinkled. "Do you even know what insurance is?"

"I know the people selling it in the shops downtown look super not-dead." Logan let his head loll back. "At the same time, your house is nice enough, Mal, but I kind of want to scratch my way right out of it."

Noah swatted Logan on the arm and threw me an apologetic glance. "Sorry. It is kind of . . . um, girly, I guess."

I shrugged. "Well, there's only girls living here, so that makes sense." I flopped back onto the bed. "There's only one jerk left, right?"

Viv's red curls bounced as she nodded her head. "The one with the long hair."

"So there's only one to worry about. I'm not going to sweat it. He's going to screw up soon enough." I was lying. All of these guys were dangerous, the monster under the bed come to terrible and fragrant life. At the same time, I was hungry, and arguing about it wasn't going to make anything better.

"The police here will find him fast." Noah nodded quickly.

"Especially if they call in the state police." Viv stood up, and I stood beside her. "Let's go grab snacks. I'm not letting them starve us into submission either."

We crept toward the dining room, only to find my mom calling for pizza. Dad had pulled his chair out a little bit away from the rest of the group, but otherwise, everyone looked pretty calm.

Dad got updates while we ate our pizza. He didn't have to share them with the rest of us, but he did and I was glad. Even though I couldn't do anything with the information—that I knew of—just knowing made me feel more empowered. "Our boy is Paul Fellowes, forty-one, most recently of the John J. Moran Medium Security Facility in Cranston, Rhode Island." He peered over at me and my friends. "That's a prison. Stay out of it.

"Apparently, he has a record for armed robbery, aggravated assault, armed home invasion, and grand theft auto. Isn't that cute? He skipped town before beginning a sentence for yet another aggravated assault conviction, this one with a hate crime designation. Awesome." He looked up from his phone. "And these are the people you want around our kids?"

"No one *wants* them around our kids, Fred." Mrs. McCrory had the tone of someone who'd said the same thing so often she didn't need to think about it anymore—like a mom, really. "We're just not willing to let them control our lives indefinitely. I assume he's going to stay in jail?"

Dad made a face. "Like the others, the judge deemed him to be a flight risk. I expect he'll be returning to scenic Cranston before facing charges here, which is just fine. I also expect he'll be entering the maximum security facility there."

"Why are all the jails in Rhode Island in Cranston?" I scratched my head.

"It's not that big a state, sweetheart." Mom dropped a kiss onto my head. "Might as well keep everything contained, am I right?”

“I guess. It’s probably got something to do with supplies, right?”

“Exactly. So the other two also have ties to Rhode Island.” Mom glanced back at Dad.

“Don’t start, Lil. You’re out of the business and this isn’t one of your books.”

The other parents all rolled their eyes, in sync. I honestly wondered if they’d arranged it beforehand.

“So you’ll be having some down time, I assume.” Mr. McCrory took a bite out of his pizza. “It’s not like you can do your job with that thing on your wrist.”

“We’ll see about that.” Dad curled his lip, and then he sighed. “They’re making me take two weeks off, and we’ll see how the X-ray looks after that. I hate it, but that’s the rule. I don’t know if I can manage it with these thugs out there though.” His good hand shook as he lifted his pizza to his lip. “I’ll be staying here to keep an eye on things, obviously.”

I froze in midbite. It wasn’t that I didn’t love my dad. It was just that him living here with my mom, under the same roof, would result in the kind of explosion people would write stories about for generations to come.

“Oh my God.” Mrs. McCrory covered her mouth.

“It’s not negotiable.” Dad glared at everyone in turn. “They’ve found everyplace else—even broke into a cop’s house looking for you kids. I have to keep you safe.”

“They found us by the names, Dad.” I managed to swallow the bite of pizza that lay on my tongue. It was hard work, but I managed it. “They’re more likely to go for Nan and Grandda, because they’re Cavans.”

All the color drained from Dad’s face. “Excuse me.”

He pushed his chair away from the table. "I need to make a phone call."

CHAPTER TWENTY

Mom had saved us all from living under constant lockdown, but we weren't out of the woods yet. While Dad got settled in with Nan and Grandda, we still had to face the fact that someone was probably coming after us. We were safer with Mom because of the whole name thing, but *safer* didn't mean *safe*. We couldn't let our guard down. Things kind of settled down for the next few days though. We spent a pretty quiet weekend at home, and in some ways it was like going away to a beach house. There was no beach, but we set up a kiddie pool in the backyard and Mr. Snuffles sat in it when the sun got too hot for him. Noah and I practiced puck handling, and Logan and Viv played basketball on the pavement. It was behind a tall fence, so no one could see us from the street, even if we could see out.

It would have been kind of nice, if we didn't see a cop car driving by every half hour.

We didn't spend the whole time splashing in the kiddie pool and playing sports. Sometimes, we sat around and talked, whether that was outside in the killer sun or inside watching old hockey games. The adults spent plenty of time talking, and I guess we could have joined them if we wanted to.

We didn't need them telling us not to think about things though or not to get involved. We were already involved, and the only way to get uninvolved would be for the drug dealers to go away. So we kept to ourselves.

"What I still don't get is what any of this has to do with the treasure." Noah sat with his feet on my wall, and his back on the floor. I'd come to think of this as his "thinking" pose. He looked ridiculous, but it wasn't a new look for him.

"It doesn't have anything to do with any treasure. I told you that ten times already. It's just a coincidence." I tossed a pillow at him, but without much heat behind it.

Both twins were clinging to this idea that the drug dealers were looking for the treasure, and I guessed I could understand that.

"It can't be a coincidence. It's too . . . it's too neat, you know?" He sat up and looked right at me. "They just happen to show up when the museum gets robbed? It doesn't make sense."

"You don't think guys like that have ever been to a museum." Viv scoffed. "And come on, the museum never had treasure."

"Then what is it we found in the woods? The gems and stuff?" Logan stopped going through the pens and pencils on my desk and turned to face the rest of us. "Mac and cheese?"

"You're the one who realized drug dealers hide stuff in other stuff." Noah waggled his eyebrows at me. "Come on, Mal, you already figured it out."

"Yeah, I figured out that it was a coincidence. I don't know what's up with the gems. I saw them too, but they're not anything to do with the creeps." I shook my head. "Seriously, don't you think the museum would have made a big display from the treasure?"

"Not if they didn't want people to steal it." Noah smirked, smug and secure in his explanation. "Which they wound up doing anyway."

Viv just gave him this look, the kind that said how much she pitied him. "The sun has baked your brains."

"You're just jealous because we can go out into the sun without turning into a giant freckle, and neither of you can." Noah stuck his tongue out at her.

"Hey—I *like* Viv's freckles." Logan punched his brother in the arm, and the whole conversation disintegrated into a brawl between the twins. Most things did, eventually.

Later, I managed to catch Mom in a private moment and gave her an extra hug. "Thanks for making sure we could get a few hours with more than just the twins for company."

She laughed and gave me a squeeze. "Hey—I've got your back."

I've never been so grateful for Monday to roll around, but when it did, I almost threw a party. We piled into our separate cars and all headed to the rink, where we suited up just like every day. Viv sat up in the bleachers with the adults and Mr. Snuffles, who really didn't like to watch games but put up with it anyway. The rest of us hit the ice.

"What's it like living with the Terrible Twosome?" My friend Megan, the goalie, skated up to me between drills. "Is it weird?"

"So weird. I mean they're not as bad as I thought

they'd be, but they're just like they are here. We'll be going along all normal and stuff, and then a fistfight breaks out." I shook my head. "What's up with that?"

"I have brothers." She nodded sagely. "And boy cousins. It's normal. Sometimes, you can use a bucket of cold water to separate them."

"My mom would actually kill me if I dumped a bucket of cold water in her house." I glanced up at Mom, who waved cheerfully.

The twins were punching each other again.

"It could be worth it though." I turned back to Megan, who laughed.

"A spray bottle might be just as good."

Coach blew the whistle, and we got back to work.

We played our scrimmage, with me playing against the twins this time, and I won't pretend I wasn't pleased to knock them both on their butts. After the scrimmage, we all headed to the dressing room to get out of our pads and head home.

I hadn't exactly been all blasé about safety. I'd stayed home instead of going to the beach, the library, or anyplace else. I'd let the stupid Scott twins live in my house. I'd paid attention to my surroundings. I listened to the adults, who worked in the crime business and knew how crooks operated. All of them believed the creeps wouldn't dare come back to the rink.

Even experts can be wrong. The creep with the long hair was standing in the dressing room when we walked in, and as soon as the last of his targets walked in, he closed and locked the door.

About half of my age group was in the locker room at this point. Other kids were outside, banging on the door.

156

Long Hair grabbed someone's stick to bolt the door shut, so even if someone could find a key, they still couldn't get in.

We were still in our skates.

There was another door, and for half a second, I thought we might be able to get through it. I turned toward it, but Long Hair had already taken care of it. Two hockey sticks bolted it shut, and I could see the lock had already been turned.

Long Hair grabbed Megan, who'd barely gotten her helmet off. She was the smallest of all of us, and her skin took on a green tinge when she took a deep breath.

Long Hair pulled a knife from somewhere; I hadn't noticed it when he showed up. My heart rate had been up from the scrimmage, but now, it jumped into overtime.

"You little punks are going to give me what I came for. I want the cash. If you don't give me the cash, I'm going to cut it out of your little friend's skin, piece by piece." He grinned, showing a mouth full of blackened and rotting teeth.

Megan set her jaw. Her pupils were tiny, and I knew she had to be terrified. After all, some unshowered guy had lifted her up off the ground and threatened her.

But hockey players are tough as nails. Girl hockey players are tougher, and goalies? Well, goalies are made of something not found on Planet Earth. Megan met my eyes and kicked backward into Long Hair's thigh.

With her skate on.

Her razor-sharp skate.

Long Hair shouted a curse and dropped her. She landed on her hands and knees, but she knew how to move fast in a position like that. She had to, if she wanted to cover pucks.

"Now!" I yelled. I grabbed my stick and used it like a spear, driving it into his sternum as hard as I could. Noah wielded his like an axe, bringing it down onto Long Hair's unprotected head, and Noah slammed his into Long Hair's knee.

Other players scrambled around us. Someone unlocked the door to the ice. Someone else got the door to the lobby open. Another person—a girl, I noticed with pride—got the knife away by punching the bad guy's wrist until he let go.

Adults flowed into the locker room, like a dam had burst and now they could flood the unsuspecting town underneath. I tossed my gloves and went to punch the smelly guy on the ground, but someone pulled me off him.

All around me, the same thing was happening with everyone else. The creep lunged to his feet and staggered out toward the lobby. No one stopped him as he climbed into a gold-colored Honda.

Mom wrapped me up in her arms. It took me a minute to register what was happening, and then I relaxed into it. "I kind of smell like hockey," I told her, like she didn't already know.

A pool of blood on the dressing room floor was all that remained of Long Hair's little stunt.

"I know, honey." She took my helmet off for me. Her hands shook. "Are you okay?"

Mr. Snuffles strode over to the pool of blood. He sniffed it and started barking right away.

One of the other hockey parents, pale and sweaty, turned to our side of the room. "Someone get that mutt under control!"

Mom stood to her full height. "This *mutt* is a police K-9, thank you."

I went over to Mr. Snuffles and got my hand under his collar. "Hey, buddy. It's okay. Stand down." It wasn't his fault we already knew where Long Hair had gone. And while Mr. Snuffles was only following his training, I could see where the barking would get on the last nerve of someone who'd also just gotten the scare of a lifetime.

I heard sirens in the distance, but Lt. Ramos beat them there. He must have broken the laws of physics to get to the rink before anyone else. He chased us out of the dressing room and made us get out of our pads and skates in the lobby, where he could see anyone coming or going. He also took my statement, and Megan's, personally.

"Whoever they're working for must be pretty mad to send him back into the rink, where he knew they'd be protected." He grimaced at Megan. "I think it's obvious we're going to need to swab your skates, sweetheart."

"Whatever you need." She looked away. "Would that guy have really hurt me?"

He opened his mouth. Then he closed it again. "Anything's possible. The important thing is you were able to defend yourself, you and the other kids. I'm proud of you. You're strong, okay?"

She didn't look like she believed him. She looked like she wanted to throw up. "I can't believe I let him grab me."

"He's bigger, stronger, and you had no reason to think he was going to do something like that. The important thing is, you're here now, telling your story, and he's running off bleeding. Right?" Lt. Ramos caught her eye and held it.

Megan stood up a little straighter. "Yeah. Yeah, that's right."

"Good girl. And the rest of your team stood up for you too, right?"

She grinned now. "That's right. They did. Mallory got him good right in the chest." She patted herself in the middle of the chest, right where I'd gotten Long Hair. "He's not going to forget how he got his butt kicked by a bunch of kids."

"No, he won't." Ramos grinned. "You give me a call if anything comes up, even if a potted plant is out of place and it makes you nervous, okay?" He gave Megan and her mom cards.

Then he escorted those of us who were living with my mom to our cars. "The getaway car is a new development. He's gotten help. I don't know if the other person was local or no, but it's an issue."

"The car had Rhode Island plates." Mr. Scott ran a hand through his hair. "I couldn't get the whole plate number, but it did have Rhode Island plates."

"That's helpful. We can put out a BOLO for that. With any luck, it will help us find him." Ramos ruffled my hair. "I'm going to go peel Fred off the ceiling now."

I was beyond happy Lt. Ramos had to do that and not me and Mom.

CHAPTER TWENTY-ONE

Aunt Teresa and Aunt Clara came over to the house as soon as we got home. I wasn't sure how they heard about the attack, but they did and they headed to the house as soon as they did. Mom's house was all but bursting at the seams now. We had the four of us kids, the McCrorys, Mr. Scott, Mom, Lt. Ramos, and now my aunts all hanging around in various parts of a house that was never meant to contain quite so many people.

Of course, Aunt Teresa could fill a house all by herself.

I expected Dad to show up in a huff, and I think that's why Lt. Ramos was there too. Maybe Dad wasn't supposed to be driving, or maybe he was afraid Long Hair would show up for his parents. Either way, he stayed where he was and limited himself to a few terse words to my mother by phone.

Or maybe I should say she limited him to a few terse words, since she hung up on him.

Aunt Teresa was in rare form. "I don't understand how the government can manage to track their unwitting guinea pigs in the MK Ultra program but can't find one smelly miscreant running through a small town where everyone knows each other." She sniffed and gave Lt. Ramos her best suspicious glower. "Too busy running interference for QAnon?"

Lt. Ramos stared at her. "I've seen your show online, but I honestly believed it was all an act." He turned to me. "Is she for real?"

"I'm never a hundred percent sure." I offered him a bowl of grapes. Mom was very firm about showing hospitality, even in times like this. "Fruit?"

Aunt Teresa winked at me. "It's best not to let them know, sweetheart. Keeps them on their toes." Then, while I tried to figure out what on earth she could possibly mean by that, she turned back to Lt. Ramos. "So tell me, what exactly are you bozos doing to try to keep our kids safe? This guy managed to sneak into the rink and take a child hostage. That's not safe."

Mom put her hand on Teresa's shoulder. "No one expected them to be stupid enough to try to come back to the rink, honestly. And while I'm not thrilled about it, the fact that he did it at all gives us a vital clue."

"What's that?" Mr. Scott massaged his temples, which had started to turn gray in only a few days. "So far the only clue we have is that he smells bad and probably comes from Rhode Island. That doesn't exactly narrow it down, especially in July."

Mr. McCrory made a rude gesture us kids probably weren't supposed to see. "I'm from Rhode Island."

"And you seem to have discovered soap. I'm proud of you, Doc, but seriously—"

"The clue," I said loudly, before they could get even ruder, "is in the heap of blood on the ground." I looked over at Lt. Ramos to see if I was right. "If he was in jail in

Rhode Island, he'll have had his DNA tested, right?"

Lt. Ramos nodded, with a little grin. "That's true, Mallory. Ordinarily, we'd have a pretty big backlog of evidence and it would have to wait, but the fact that he tried to take a child hostage bumps him to the top of the list. We still won't get an ID for a couple of days, but it's a start."

"It still doesn't tell us where he is." Mrs. McCrory grimaced and reached for a glass of water.

"It could." Aunt Clara tapped her fingers against the table. "You know, if it shows he's got family in the area. It would explain the getaway driver."

"If he's got family in the area, why couldn't he shower?" Noah scratched the side of his nose. "I'm just saying. People remember weird things about other people. No one would think twice about a guy with long hair. It's a little weird, but it's not something that stands out that much. The stink though?"

Lt. Ramos gave Noah an encouraging smile. "You've got a good point, son. And that's an important thing to pick up on. People do remember things that stand out, and especially things that stand out in bad ways."

Someone knocked on the door while Noah preened.

My heart kicked into a whole different gear. I jumped in front of Viv and Mr. Snuffles. The grown-ups all paled. Mrs. McCrory dropped her fork.

Lt. Ramos got up, hand on his gun. "I'll answer this one."

He crept over to the door while the rest of us waited in total silence. Then he took a position against the wall and threw the door open with his non-gun hand.

Jimmy Flannigan, the guy who owned the rink, stood there with his jaw hanging open.

"Is everything okay here?" He looked around, eyes wide.

Lt. Ramos stepped into view. His hand was still on his gun. "Is anyone with you today, Jimmy?"

Mr. Flannigan shook his head. "Well, no. Why would they be?" He tugged at his collar. "I was hoping I could have a talk with Mrs. Cavan. You know, private-like."

"It's Ms. Corwin, thank you." Aunt Clara's face tightened into a weird mask. I imagined she looked like this in court—cold, emotionless, and ready to tear someone apart if they crossed her.

Maybe lawyering could be a good backup career once hockey was over with.

Mr. Flannigan swallowed hard. "Right. Sorry. Er, Ms. Corwin?"

Mom sighed. "Come on in and join the party, Jimmy." She gestured to the table. "I'm afraid we're fresh out of private, under the circumstances."

"Right." Mr. Flannigan walked in.

Lt. Ramos closed the door behind him.

"So what brings you buy, Jimmy? Help yourself to some fruit." Mom gave him a tired smile.

There weren't any free seats. Us kids were already sitting on the floor. Mr. Flannigan had to stand near my mom's right hand, between her and Lt. Ramos. It must have felt at least kind of intimidating, especially with my aunts glaring daggers at him.

Mr. Flannigan took a deep breath and took off his red ball cap. "Look. I'll get right to it. I wouldn't ask this under normal circumstances." He glanced at Mr. Scott. "I'd have come to see you too, but it looks like I've already found you. I've got to ask a favor."

Mom raised an eyebrow. "All things considered, it's got to be a pretty big ask."

Mr. Flannigan flushed scarlet for a moment, but he kept his voice down. "I have to ask you to pull Mallory and the twins from hockey camp for the rest of the summer."

"What? No!" I only realized after I heard the words echoing off the walls that they'd come from my own mouth. I didn't remember getting back to my feet either.

"You can't do that to us!" Noah stood on my right side. "Tell them, Dad!"

"We didn't do anything!" Logan stood on my left.

Mr. Flannigan sighed and twisted his hat in his hands. "I understand that. But there've been two incidents where other children were put in danger, and it's all centered around you three. It might not be your fault, but it's still about you and it's your responsibility. I have other kids to think about. Don't you care that some jerk took Megan hostage today?"

Guilt surged up from my gut, but anger tamped it down. "And how did he get in there, huh?" I tossed my hair over my shoulder. "There are cops patrolling the place, all the parents know what he looks like. So how did he get into the rink?"

"The getaway driver." Mom laughed, but there wasn't any humor in it. "The getaway driver works for the rink. He must have let him in through a back door, so he didn't have to go through the crowded lobby or get seen by parents." She shook her head. "Means he has to have local help."

"Look, everyone at the rink has been working for me for years." Mr. Flannigan scowled and braced himself on the table, leaning forward. "They're my friends and family. I've known them forever. None of those guys would let some drug dealer onto the property."

Lt. Ramos pursed his lips and scratched his chin, like he was calmly thinking about it. "So since you're so sure your guys are clean you'll have no problem coming down to the station with a list of all your employees from, say, the past two years?"

"I don't have to do that." Mr. Flannigan stood up straight and crossed his arms over his chest. "I came here to ask Mrs. Cavan—"

"Ms. Corwin." Aunt Clara interrupted him with a voice like a knife.

"Ms. Corwin to do the right thing and pull her kid, for the safety of everyone. If she won't do it voluntarily, I'll expel her for good—and I do mean for good."

Aunt Clara cracked her knuckles. "I see. And when you do that, of course, you'll be opening yourself up to a delightful little lawsuit I'm already drawing up. I texted one of my paralegals in the office, and she started the paperwork here while you were speaking, so I won't have any trouble heading to the courthouse to file it once you leave." She smiled sweetly. "Coming here to intimidate witnesses, while blaming child victims for your own negligence? For shame, Mr. Flannigan. For shame."

"See here—I'm not doing anything wrong." Mr. Flannigan turned white as a sheet.

"I find it fascinating that a business owner would rather attack child victims of crime than stand by them and cooperate with an investigation into how the crime happened in the first place." Aunt Teresa pulled out her phone and held it out. I noticed a red dot blinking on the screen. She was recording. "Tell me, Mr. Flannigan. More to the point, tell my audience. What are you hiding? Who are you working with?"

He swayed on his feet. "Look. There's no need to be hasty here."

"Hm." Aunt Clara raised her eyebrow. "If you didn't want people to be hasty, you shouldn't have come here to try to intimidate scared parents and children into giving up something that they need right now. As it is, your best-case scenario is that Liliana comes out of this owning your rink. Want to keep digging?"

Mom looked over at Mrs. McCrory. "Do I want a rink?"

Mrs. McCrory shrugged. "Does it matter?"

Mr. Flannigan threw his hands up. "Look. Forget I said anything." He turned on his heel and tried to leave, but Lt. Ramos grabbed him by the shoulder.

"Sorry, Jimmy. There's still that matter of how the suspect got into the rink that we need to talk about."

He radioed to headquarters to send someone else to keep an eye on us while he brought Mr. Flannigan in to discuss matters. The rest of us sat in silence while he drove away.

I'm not sure what was going through anyone else's mind. I know how I was feeling. On the one hand, we had our first real lead since this whole thing started. On the other, if Long Hair had friends on the staff at the rink, we were in trouble for the rest of time. Maybe we should have let Mr. Flannigan ban us for life. It might have been safer.

"So." Mom spoke up in an artificially bright voice.

"That happened."

Mr. Scott blew out a long breath. "Yeah. You think they got to him?"

Aunt Teresa shook her head and turned off her phone. "No. I think he's a small-minded jerk who's just trying to limit bad publicity for his business." She chuckled quietly. "I had a few dates with him once, a long time ago. He hasn't changed. But he doesn't get to come here and try to guilt or intimidate my niece or my sister, or the people staying with them." She shrugged.

"I might file the lawsuit anyway." Clara shrugged. "The guy's a pig."

Mom held her hands up. "Let's hold that option in reserve, Clara. Right now, I'll be happy if we can just find out where this creep is hiding and bring him down."

CHAPTER TWENTY-TWO

The Corwin sisters managed to keep us in hockey camp, but I couldn't be sure exactly when that would change. So far, the other parents had been pretty cool. They understood it wasn't our fault. Eventually that might change, and I understood that. I knew it wasn't our fault that the creeps were coming after us, but if I was a parent it wouldn't matter. I wouldn't want my kid in danger no matter whose fault it was.

And if the creeps were bringing other kids into it, like Megan, then everyone in hockey camp was in danger.

"I'm not okay with this." I tossed a stress ball into the air and caught it. "It's just . . . it's stupid. I don't want to just spend my life sitting around and waiting for these jerks to attack again."

"Now you know what it's like to be a goalie." Logan wagged his eyebrows at me. "Only in this scenario you're the guy with long hair."

I wanted to argue, but he was right. "My teeth are better," I told him instead. "And I smell better."

"Not after hockey you don't." Viv held her nose. "Yuck."

I stuck my tongue out at her. "You all know exactly

what I mean though. I'm just waiting for someone else to do something. It's like I'm some kind of princess in a tower, waiting for a knight on a horse."

Noah scratched his head. "Isn't that what girls are supposed to want?"

Viv and I both gave him looks that should have killed him. "No," we said, in unison.

At least he staggered back.

"What do you want to do though?" Logan stood up. "They're big scary drug dealers. They have weapons. We're kids; we're watched every second of every day. And, honestly, we should be. It's annoying as heck, but I want to live long enough to make it to high school."

"Why?" Viv wrinkled her nose at him. "From everything I've seen, high school looks pretty awful."

"It can't be worse than middle school." Logan shuddered, and we all joined in. Logan wasn't right often, but when he was, he was spot on.

"The whole point is, if I had patience to be a goalie, I'd have done it back in Mites." I had to get this conversation back on track. "It improves my chances of making it to the NHL, because they've already had one female goalie."

"She played in one exhibition game." Noah tossed a grape at me. "Don't sell yourself short."

I shrugged and ate the grape. He had a point. "Still, it's better than no one ever making it. And that's not the point. The point is I can't just sit here and wait for the bad guys to do something. For one thing, it's kind of killing me here. For another, it's not working."

Viv winced. "I hate to admit it but you're right. I trust our parents, and the police, but the fact is it's not helping. They've done everything they can, and that big jerk still got into the locker room."

We all nodded quietly. The fact that Long Hair had gotten into the locker room bothered me on a deep level. It shouldn't have happened, because the police were watching the rink. It meant someone at the rink was helping him. Someone at the rink, someone who knew us, was willing to see us hurt or worse.

"What can we do though? The grown-ups can get into the security cameras. They can interrogate everyone at that rink until they talk. They can actually arrest people and send them back to Rhode Island to do . . . whatever it is they do in Rhode Island, I have no idea. We can hit them with our hockey sticks when they see us, and then we can hide in your basement again, Mal. And to be honest, it's getting a little ripe in here."

"So quit eating cheese, Logan." Noah made a rude gesture at his brother. "You're eleven years old, you'd think you'd have learned by now."

"I'm talking about your feet, stink-face."

"Well, obviously that's not what we should be talking about, since even Dad thought something got down here and died last night."

I looked at Viv. She rolled her eyes at me. Sometimes, the twins were great. Sometimes, it was like talking to a wall. I could suddenly understand why my mom had decided to stay single.

"Anyway." I raised my voice, just a little. "Yeah, we're kids. And we've got some disadvantages. But I just can't keep sitting here waiting when nothing anyone's doing is keeping me any safer. This jerk is able to hide, he's got someone local helping him. He's making all the choices. If we make him come out when we know our parents can grab him . . ." I trailed off and hoped their imaginations would do the rest of the work for me.

Noah figured it out first. "No way. First of all, there's no way they'd go for it. Second, how do we get the word *to him*? Call him on his phone?" He held his hand up to his face like it was a cell phone. "Hey, Mr. Drug Dealer Creeper Dude? Yeah, this is Noah Scott, star center and ladies' man extraordinaire. Would you mind showing up at a time and place of my choosing? Oh, no reason. Awesome. Let's just meet up at Black Sails Police Department. Easier that way. Thanks ever so much for cooperating. See you soon!" He shook his head and ducked when I threw my stress ball at him.

"You're not funny. And you're not a ladies' man. You're a twerp."

Viv stepped in before things could escalate between me and Noah the way they usually did. "We can't do that, but we can be plenty loud about making plans at the rink. The other kids will help us without even knowing it."

"Did you miss the part where our parents will never go for anything even remotely like this?" Logan waved his hand. "Don't get me wrong. I completely agree with Mallory that Noah's a twerp, and isn't even remotely funny. But we have to fight to go out into the backyard right now. They're not going to let us go out and do something dangerous just to lure out the crooks."

I had to admit Logan was right once again. It hurt like burning, but the pain just spurred my creativity. "The museum!" I snapped my fingers.

Three pairs of eyes blinked back at me.

"Sorry. I'm not following you." Even Viv didn't

have my back this time.

I counted to five. "The museum is all educational and stuff, right? Well, parents *love* educational. And they're not going to believe anyone would try to come for us at the museum. It's the Black Sail Bay Museum. No one goes there unless their school makes them. So they'll absolutely write it off as safe. But because they're not stupid, they'll insist on coming with us. And I'll be pretty firm about saying I want Lt. Ramos there too, and my dad, because we just don't feel safe leaving the house without police." I put my hand on my heart and tried to look angelic.

Now Viv understood. "But we absolutely have to get out a little bit because we're at each other's throats and on each other's nerves." She laughed. "They wouldn't want to ruin team chemistry for the new school year, would they?"

Noah laughed and rubbed his hands together. "I love it."

Logan frowned and scratched the back of his neck. "I still don't get it. How exactly do we get the creep on board again?"

"Leave that up to me." I beamed. I should probably have felt guilty about feeling good when Logan was once again confused, but the familiar can be very comforting in a crisis.

Needless to say, Mom was not enthusiastic about my sudden interest in going to the museum. "You're out of your mind. I know we're all a little crowded, but it's because we have to be. There's a person out there trying to kidnap you or worse, Mallory. Try to be sensible."

I gave her my very best puppy-dog eyes. "But, Mom, it's the museum. It's educational."

She just looked at me, exasperated. "And that's another thing. Since when have you voluntarily gone to the Black Sail Bay Museum? You've tried to fake sick every year the school tried to take you there. Sorry, I'm just not buying it."

"Mom, you don't want us to grow up too scared to set foot outside the house, do you?" It was a low blow, and I hated doing that to my mom. I didn't have a choice, or at least I didn't feel like I had one at the time. "And honestly, you'll be with us the whole time. You, the McCrorys, Mr. Scott. We even want Dad and Lt. Ramos to come along with us. We want to be safe, we just want a chance to get out and stretch our legs a little bit. See something different. We're willing to do whatever we have to do to be safe while we do it."

She shook her head. "You're up to something."

"Wasn't it the museum theft that started this whole thing off?" I was really pouring it on now. "We just—we need closure, I guess. We need to see and feel that the two aren't related, just so we can truly understand that we're not to blame for this."

Mom still didn't believe me, probably because she knew me too well. She couldn't withstand me and Mrs. McCrory though, so she reached out to Dad and Lt. Ramos.

They showed up at the house together, probably because Dad needed Lt. Ramos to keep him from losing his mind. The look on his face told me he was at least suspicious about what was going on, but he didn't say any of it out loud. I could count on small favors, at least.

Mrs. McCrory was our biggest ally in the fight to get out of the house. I kind of suspect she wanted to get out too. "Look, these kids have had the fright of their lives—several times over. If they want to get out for a little bit and see something besides the rink and these walls, and they're willing to do it safely, I say we let them. It's not like they're asking to go hiking alone in the state park. They're asking for a closely guarded and monitored trip to the most boring museum in Massachusetts. I don't think anything can go wrong there."

"Something went wrong at the rink after we thought that was safe." Dad glared at Mom, like it was somehow her fault. "How can you think it won't happen again?"

"It's *the museum*." Mrs. McCrory spread her hands wide. "The drug dealers have probably never even been in a museum before, and this one has a whole new surveillance system thanks to the whole mess with the break-in. They're desperate, but the fact that they've avoided capture this long tells me they're not *this* stupid. Let's go and see what happens."

Mom raised an eyebrow. "And if they come after us?"

"Then Fred and Lt. Ramos get to arrest them!"

Lt. Ramos turned to look directly at me. His brown eyes bored into mine, and there was no doubt in my mind that he knew. He knew exactly what we had planned. There was no getting around it.

He didn't rat us out though. Instead, he turned to our parents. "I'll admit it does seem a little unusual, but this whole situation is unusual. And we're not going to be subtle about going with these kids. It seems natural enough that they'd want to go see the museum after all the publicity from finding that one clue. I think the risk to them is low.

It's not zero, but it's low, and it does get them out of the house."

I wanted to jump up and do a jig, but I didn't. I kept my dignity until I was alone in my room with Viv later that night.

The first part of my plan was in place. I was going to need the other kids in hockey camp to make the rest work.

CHAPTER TWENTY-THREE

Megan was the only person not living in my house who got to know about what we were doing. I figured she was steady enough to keep it quiet, being a goalie and all. Plus, after being used as a hostage by the smelliest criminal in Massachusetts history, she deserved to know that someone was working on getting rid of the guy who'd grabbed her. She looked awful, with big dark circles under her eyes and skin as pale as the ice we skated on. When I told her what we were planning though, she got a grim little smile on her face. "Good. I hope you get him and finish what we started."

I almost flinched at that. She'd kicked him with her skates on, basically with knives strapped to her feet. She'd left a massive gash in his thigh. Then again, who was I to make judgments? Long Hair had grabbed her and pulled a knife. I'd have been terrified. If she was feeling a little bloodthirsty, who could possibly blame her?

"Here's what I need from you." I pushed any misgivings aside. "I need you to talk it up, while you're here. Tell everyone we're going to the museum on Saturday. We'll probably be there in the afternoon, since no one wants to see my mom before she's had at least two cups of coffee and honestly Dad's no better."

She shuddered. "You don't have to tell me twice. Remember when your mom showed up to a six a.m. game and thought Coach was a coroner?"

I had to laugh, even though our situation was nothing to laugh about. "To be fair, our coach that year did smell a little dead. He should have washed his gear more."

"Heresy!" She managed a little giggle. "I'll get the word out, don't worry." She winked at me, and we skated off to our own drills.

I wasn't sure how many people heard about our planned trip, but a few of the girls approached and asked me if I was scared to go. So at least some people heard. I had to hope it was enough.

Saturday rolled around, and it brought the first rain we'd had since Mom got back from Spain with it. It seemed like the perfect day to do something like go to the museum. I'd have preferred the library, but our parents would have known something was fishy if either of the twins voluntarily walked into the library. Besides, there were too many places for Long Hair to hide in the library. The museum was safer.

The Black Sail Bay Museum was a massive place, right on the edge of the town forest. It wasn't hard to see why the thieves had chosen to flee by cutting through the woods. Once upon a time, the museum building had been an armory. Time had passed, and someone in Washington figured out that maybe not every puny coastal town needed to have an armory. That's how the town got the building, which was all well and good, but it still had the kind of massive rooms used for tanks and stuff.

The front entrance was just such a space. If you

tried, you could just picture it being full of tanks instead of big wall-sized dividers with line drawings of vaguely Native American people and the occasional display of Native artifacts. The place was arranged so visitors moved through Black Sail Bay history, starting with the people who were here first.

It sounded great—on paper. I just never really trusted the front room, considering how little information they seemed to be willing to back up.

Anyway, we moved through the front room to the Early Colonial Room, back when Black Sail Bay was called New Chard. The museum had plenty of documentation about this, and more *stuff* too. Apparently, our ancestors—my ancestors specifically, on Mom's side—wrote a lot of things down and never threw away anything that could be useful. The museum had a whole reconstructed house, complete with mannequins supposed to look like the early colonial settlers sitting around dourly eating gruel.

And a guy in the stocks, out on the lawn, because who doesn't keep stocks on the front lawn?

Ordinarily I'd be cracking jokes with Viv or trying to put one of the Scott twins into the stocks. We'd all seen the exhibit a thousand times before, and the chances of anything new being shown here were slim to none. Today I couldn't even ask Mom why people had stocks on their lawn—something I kept meaning to do.

Every muscle in my body was tense, like in the seconds before face-off. I flinched at every sound, and I wasn't the only one. The last time Long Hair came for us, he'd brought a knife. Was he going to bring a gun this time? We were as safe as we could possibly be under the circumstances, but there was still a chance that this could go south in a hurry.

I took a breath. If things went bad, they went bad. My dad was here. So was Lt. Ramos. So was Mom, and if Long Hair was smart he was more afraid of her than he was of two armed cops and a police dog.

We passed through the Early Colonial Exhibit and moved into the Pirate Era Room. This was the weirdest room, as far as I was concerned. It had always been weird, and it was even weirder now. The walls were covered with a mural of the harbor, filled with ships, and ocean sounds played over cleverly hidden speakers. The carefully preserved bow of an actual ship—or maybe it was a reproduction, I have no idea—stuck out from the middle of the wall with the windows, complete with a figurehead of a mermaid with an open mouth and no shirt on.

Noah and Logan snickered every time they saw it. This was no exception.

This room had plenty of display cases, all with neat little cards explaining what we were looking at. Some of them contained coins, showing us the currencies in use in New Chard at the time. Others showed manacles or chains—some used for pirates taken prisoner, some used to hold the enslaved human cargo occasionally brought through the port. Bottles of rum and barrels of molasses, bolts of fabric—I'm sure it was all very historic. Maybe I'd care if I were a history student or going to write a book about pirates or something.

I was going to be a hockey player. None of the display cases showed anything that could be interpreted as a puck.

I nudged Viv. She paled a little, but we moved slowly away from our parents' sides. We had to do it carefully, so they wouldn't notice. Even Long Hair wouldn't attack if we were right up close with them. Lt. Ramos might be in plainclothes, but Long Hair knew we were associated with cops.

We still had plenty of space to get through. Long Hair could get to us from anywhere in the museum. I wanted to get our adults used to the idea of us being more than an arm's length away though, so we started it then.

Mr. Snuffles started to bark.

I looked up. So did everyone else. Long Hair and a guy who looked like Steve the Zamboni driver at the rink were running for the emergency exit, the one with the alarm on it. Lt. Ramos was already running after them. So were my mom and dad.

"Freeze! Police!" Lt. Ramos' voice echoed through the otherwise empty museum.

I went to chase after them, but Mrs. McCrory grabbed me and pulled me back with the rest of them. Her hand trembled. Mr. McCrory and Mr. Scott stood in front of us, blocking us from anyone who might attack, as a loud siren threatened to burst our eardrums.

Oh, right. The emergency exit had an alarm. I'd noticed that.

We stayed where we were, despite a computerized voice advising us to leave the building in an orderly fashion, for twenty minutes. Then the alarm stopped and Mom came back for us.

She dropped to her knees and threw her arms around me. "It's over," she whispered, squeezing me tight. "We've got them."

She looked up at the other adults. "We've got them," she said again. And then, "And with the stuff they had on them, attempted child abduction is the least of the charges they'll be looking at."

"We can go home?" Mr. McCrory perked up. "Not that I don't appreciate your hospitality, but . . ."

"But you're allergic to cats?" Mom got to her feet and grinned. She kept a firm hand on my shoulder. "I get it. I like entertaining, and I like all of you. No one likes entertaining under the gun like that."

Then Mom turned to me. Her smile was sweet, but the glint in her eyes was wicked. "But first, let's finish the museum tour. We're here, after all, and it's such a rainy day."

My friends and I exchanged glances. We couldn't complain, not without admitting we'd set the whole thing up.

And so we had to go through every boring inch of the museum. In my case, I do mean every boring inch. Mom insisted on showing me each and every artifact on display, every dull explanatory placard, and every molasses-slow exhibit. I could feel my brain rotting and leaking through my ears. The section about the name change from New Chard to Black Sail Bay alone took up a whole room, and Mom made me read the actual proclamation out loud to everyone.

With that same sweet smile on her face.

We couldn't leave until we'd gone through the whole thing, and she didn't drop the act until she got me alone in the car.

"You knew." I didn't have to explain more for her to admit it.

"Heck yes I knew. I suspected when you actually said you wanted to go to the museum." She sighed, and she seemed to deflate. I noticed she had a few cuts on her knuckles, like she'd punched someone or something. Had she gotten into a fistfight with Long Hair?

"What you did, Mallory, was incredibly dangerous. You had no way of knowing if they had guns. You put all of us at risk." Then she took a deep breath. "I understand why you did it though."

"You do?" I blinked a few times.

"Yeah. I do. You were feeling like . . . like everything was outside of your control. Like this guy was calling all the shots, right? He was making all the plays, and someone took away your stick so you couldn't do anything to stop him. Heck, you guys were right there when Mr. Flannigan threatened to boot you from hockey camp."

I gaped at her, unable to find the words. Mom hadn't even watched hockey before I decided I wanted to play. How was it possible that she understood exactly what was going on in my head?

"These were very dangerous men. I don't like . . ." She drifted off, pressing her mouth shut. "I don't like you putting yourself in danger like that. I hate it, in fact. That said, you were already in danger. Just do me a favor and promise me you won't set any more traps for a bunch of drug runners who want to hurt you, okay?"

I nodded, eyes down. "I promise." I could have argued, I guess, but why? Mom already knew what was going through my head. She said she understood. She *did* understand. "I love you, Mom."

She laughed now and ruffled my hair. "I love you, Mallory. And I'm proud of you. Now let's go home and get back to having our house to ourselves."

CHAPTER TWENTY-FOUR

I'm not normally the most enthusiastic person when it comes to house cleaning. Mom will probably be the first person to tell you this, not that she's got any room to complain. She pays other people to come and do it, most of the time. Once we got home from the museum though, we both got to work scrubbing the house from head to toe. We didn't even talk about it. We just did it.

It's not that our guests were dirty people. Okay, Noah and Logan were pretty dirty, but that's just normal for eleven-year-old boys. Maybe, just maybe, you could make a case for it being normal for all eleven-year-old hockey players.

But Viv, and her parents, and Mr. Scott? They're all perfectly normal, clean people. The only thing is, now the whole house smelled like other people. Nice people, people who were our friends, but still other people.

My aunts showed up to help. I don't know how they knew. I know for a fact Dad didn't call them. If they hadn't shown up, we'd have been at it until midnight, so I'm glad they came over. As it was, the sun had set before we called for a pizza.

My mom's sisters didn't look much alike, most of

the time. Aunt Clara, the oldest, had blonde hair, and she was usually dressed for court—even on Saturdays. Today though, she wore jeans and a T-shirt. Her hair was pulled back into a regular ponytail and partially hidden under a bandana too. Aunt Teresa, the youngest, had her dark hair under a bandana like Clara's. She wore a tank top with her show's logo on it.

All three sisters slouched in their chairs at the kitchen table, little grins on their faces despite their fatigue. "Never, ever, tell Mom I came over and voluntarily scrubbed a floor." Aunt Teresa wagged a finger at both of her older sisters.

Mom snorted. "That would mean admitting I cleaned my own house. She'd be too happy about that. I could never." She took a bite of her pizza and all three of them laughed.

I relaxed into the feeling. For the first time since this whole thing started, I felt safe and secure. The drug dealers were gone, they were going to jail in Rhode Island so they might as well be on the moon, and I was here in my house with my mom and my aunts.

Of course, when that thought occurred to me, something else popped into my head to dim the warm glow. It could only dim it a little bit, but even that little bit chewed at the corners of my brain like a mouse. "Hey, did anyone ever figure out what happened with the museum theft?"

Mom stiffened, but then she relaxed. "I thought we talked about this, sweetheart. The museum theft and the drug dealers had nothing to do with each other. They were just coincidental."

"They were." I nodded and grabbed for another

slice of pizza. Hey, I was a growing girl and an active hockey player. I needed fuel. "I just kind of feel like everyone stopped paying attention to the museum theft once the Stinky Bandits showed up."

Clara snickered around her mouth full of food. She covered her mouth with her napkin, finished chewing, and gave me a thumbs-up. "Bonus points for the name. Would you believe that Steve from the rink had the gall to call me and ask me to defend him?"

Mom's eyes flashed dangerously. "I'm happy to go discuss the issue with him."

Teresa raised one eyebrow. "Are you suggesting he's not entitled to representation?"

"He's entitled to whatever representation he needs. He's just not entitled to ask it of anyone in Mallory's family." Mom glared at Teresa for a second, and then she stuck her tongue out at her. "Which you know."

Teresa laughed. "I know, I'm just messing with you. Fred's not here, so I have to mess with someone."

Clara nudged her. "You're welcome to call him on the phone and mess with him. Liliana's been through enough lately." She turned her attention back to Mom. "Yeah, I said basically the same thing. I did offer to call Drew Marsh from Salem, who took the case and paid me a finder's fee." She rolled her eyes. "I do family law, not criminal defense. Steve doesn't seem to be the brightest bulb on the tree, I'm afraid."

I cleared my throat. "So has there been any progress on the museum theft?" Keeping adults on task was hard work. I couldn't imagine what it might be like to have to manage them for money. Lt. Ramos must have had the patience of a saint.

Mom grabbed for her water. "Lt. Ramos said the case doesn't have many leads. This goes no further, Mallory, and I'm only telling you because you got put into a bad situation because of the whole museum mess."

Teresa cleared her throat. "It's not Dr. Edwards' fault that the drug dealers made bad choices."

"No. But his decisions did lead a bunch of people to go off 'treasure hunting,' which the drug dealers do seem to have used as a ruse to hide their activity. And the state of the storage room made it hard to tell exactly what had been stolen, which means finding the thief is next to impossible." Mom rubbed at her scraped-up knuckles.

Clara curled her lip. "Dr. Edwards' always been a bit of a ditz. And of course he's coming up roses again. Admissions at the museum are up three hundred percent, entirely because of the robbery. People are coming down from Maine, they're coming up from Boston—even tourists from New York and California are adding Black Sail Bay to their itineraries, just to see the museum that got robbed."

I pulled back a little. "That doesn't sound right. It can't be right."

"It doesn't sound fair, anyway." Mom sighed. "Don't get me wrong. The museum was having its worst year ever. I'm glad to have the revenue. It does strike me as kind of odd, but there isn't a whole lot we can do about it."

I bowed my head and wrinkled my nose. Sure, part of me knew people got away with things sometimes. Heck, I got away with things all the time because I did them when the ref wasn't looking. That's just part of hockey.

This was an adult, and instead of sneaking in a little check under the ref's nose during a game, he was messing with police time and taxpayer money. I didn't pay taxes, but I knew people who did tended to get pretty irate when folks who had access to said money misused it.

"You can fire him." I looked back up at Mom. "I mean, no one likes to put someone else out of a job, but if he's not doing his job the right way . . ."

Aunt Clara gave me a little smile. "Well, it's certainly on the table. There's a process though, exactly like there is for everything else when it comes to government jobs. The board has to meet certain criteria before we can take action."

"Also, finding someone who wants to curate a small, underfunded museum in Black Sail Bay is going to be a challenge, to say the least." Aunt Teresa grimaced and made a face at her pizza. "What's got you so upset about the museum theft, Mal? I know when I was your age I thought going to the museum was a punishment."

I blushed. Mom hadn't told them about my plot to force the Stinky Bandit out into the open, or at least I didn't think she had. "It just doesn't seem right. We know something was stolen. My friends and I found part of it. We were in the paper and everything."

"That's right, you were." Clara grinned. "And you want some resolution to the case, I guess."

"Yeah, that." Kids don't usually think in terms of *resolution*, but it sounded plausible.

"Unfortunately, I don't have anything to offer. Eventually, I hope we can get the museum into some kind of shape, but for now, I think the case is just going to have to stay open."

I nodded and went back to my pizza. Arguing about it wasn't going to get me answers, given that none of the people there with me had any to give. We'd been having such a good evening, warm and open, and I just wanted it to continue.

Deep down inside though, I had to wonder if the story didn't go deeper.

Dad came over the next day. He still looked like a bit of a mess, but the bruising on his face was starting to fade a bit and his jaw wasn't quite so tight. "I moved back into my place." He sat down on my mom's couch.

"Make yourself at home." Mom rolled her eyes.

Dad ignored her. "The guy with the long hair was Brett Carson. He was seriously bad news, with a rap sheet as long as my arm. Someone had stitched that gash your goalie friend Megan put in his thigh up with dental floss. It got infected, so they've got him locked down in the infirmary at the prison. I'm pretty sure he can't get out of there."

I let out a breath I hadn't realized I'd been holding. "You're positive?"

"As sure as I can be. He won't be going back to jail in Rhode Island. Apparently, California has priority for a different set of charges he skipped out on, so that'll be fun." He shook his head, mouth all pursed like he'd bit into a bad lemon. "I just don't get how all of these guys were able to just decide not to show up for stuff and get away with it. All the US Marshalls and bounty hunters in America couldn't bring them in, but a bunch of preteen hockey players managed to do it."

"Maybe the US Marshalls will give us a job." I grinned at my dad, knowing exactly how he'd react.

"Don't start with me, Mallory." He gave me a

baleful look.

"Say goodbye to Mr. Snuffles. He's coming with me. We're going to hunt down bad guys, using just our noses and hockey sticks."

"Mallory, don't rile your father up." Mom yawned. There was no heat in her voice. She'd said what she needed to say yesterday, and that was all there was to it. "Fred, you know she's just trying to get your goat."

Dad shook his head, but at least he stopped giving me the death glare. "It's her favorite hobby these days. I had a few words with the rink owner, and we're all set there too."

Mom raised her eyebrows, but otherwise showed no reaction.

"Has he signed the deed over to Mom yet?" Mr. Snuffles rolled over, and I rubbed his belly.

Dad blushed. "Okay, he told me if I kept my wife and my sisters-in-law off his back, he'd let the team practice there for free all year. Which—I mean, ice time is a big cost for the league."

"Did you include the girls' club team?" I tried to keep my voice casual.

"Yes, I did. He balked at that, but when I pointed out that his nephew tried to get Clara to be his defense attorney, he agreed." Dad sighed. "I never meet the smart criminals."

Steve had been Mr. Flannigan's nephew? I hadn't known that. I decided to pretend I did though. The last thing I needed was either of my parents telling me just how interconnected everything was in this town.

Mom asked about Dad's parents, and I scurried off to my room. I hadn't forgotten about the museum theft, even if everyone else seemed willing to write it off. I sent off a text to the rest of the crew who'd gone through the whole messy drug dealer affair with me.

Anyone else still want to know where the museum treasure is?

CHAPTER TWENTY-FIVE

As it turned out, Logan didn't want to know anything at all about the museum treasure. He let me know in as many terms as possible, just so I understood. He told me via text. He told me on video chat. He told me in person on Monday morning, when we all saw each other at the rink. "Was it somehow not enough of an adventure for you to get us all almost killed by a bunch of drug dealers from Rhode Island?"

Noah punched him, hard. "Dude, you're the one who was all gung-ho about the whole pirate thing in the first place. The only people responsible for what those jerks did are those jerks. If you want to blame someone for putting us where they could get to us, blame yourself."

Logan hit back because he was never someone who admitted he deserved to be punched. "Jerk! You were just as excited about pirate treasure as I was."

Noah swung back at his brother. This time he connected with Logan's jaw, and all activity in the room stopped. We were all used to them fighting. It was just part of who they were, like their apparent allergy to the letter *R* or their blue eyes. They almost never went for the face though. The face meant it was serious.

"How does that make it Mallory's fault that a bunch of creepers wanted to go after us?" Noah shouted.

I backed away, ending up closer to Megan. "Should we maybe go and get Coach?"

Megan narrowed her eyes as she watched the twins grappling on the floor. Noah seemed to have the upper hand. He swung wildly, but he was on top of Logan and didn't look like he wanted to let up any time soon.

"Nah," she said after a few minutes. "I think they're good. Besides, Noah's right. Nothing that happened is your fault." She patted me on the back, grabbed her helmet and headed out toward the ice.

After a moment, I followed. This wasn't about me. The Scott twins had been on their best behavior while they were cooped up at my house. They were bound to lose it eventually.

Mom went into the dressing room when she realized they were still in there, and she dragged them both out just in time for drills to start. Personally, I'd have let them face the consequences of being late, but maybe that's just me. They seemed to cool down by lunchtime, and by the end of camp they were acting like normal again.

Well, as normal as they ever got.

Mr. Scott had to work today, so Mom had agreed to bring us all over to the McCrorys' place to swim. I'm not sure how Viv felt about us invading her space, but I guess none of our parents were about to let us hang out by ourselves for a while. And the brothers probably shouldn't have been left alone anyway. Who knows what Mr. Scott would have come home to?

We lounged around on our inflatable floating things, which inevitably turned into pirate battles. I didn't bring up the treasure thing again because Logan had a black eye and a split lip. I didn't want to make things worse.

Viv either didn't notice or didn't care. "You know, when I saw your text last night I wasn't sure what to think. After everything, I was kind of all set on adventure. But I have to admit, I'm still curious. What happened to the treasure? And what did get stolen from the museum, anyway?"

Noah stiffened. "We know what got stolen. We found that bag of jewels and stuff, remember?"

I shrugged and tried to move my float closer to the shade, not that there was much shade out here in the pool. "Okay, but we don't know for sure that the gems were from the museum. They could have been hidden by someone else. They could have been hidden by the drug dealer creeps. It could be just a coincidence that they were out there at all. There's no record of the museum having a heap of jewels or anything like that."

"From what your mom said, there weren't great records of the museum having *anything*." Noah shook his head. "It sounds like that place is a real mess. Who knows what they've got locked away in there?"

"Okay, valid, but if it was treasure they'd have said." I stopped trying to move my little raft and just let the current move me. "I don't want to get into any more trouble with creeps or anything like that—not now, not ever, no thank you. I'd like the next thousand adults I have contact with to bathe. But the whole not knowing thing is bothering me, like when you get the straps to your pads twisted."

The boys nodded because they'd done it too. Viv looked at me kind of blankly for a long moment, and then she shrugged. She didn't have to understand the sensation, because she knew exactly how I felt. She knew me better than anyone else.

"You hate not knowing things." She chuckled and used her hands like paddles, so she could move her float closer to me. "But think about it, Mal—we don't have anything to go on. There's no way our parents are going to let us go digging around for treasure again, not after what happened last time. And I'm about a thousand percent not up for doing it on our own, you know? Not after everything."

"Yeah, hard pass. And I'm pretty sure there's not even a real treasure anyway." I glanced over at our moms, who were chatting on deck chairs. I didn't think they were listening, but moms can be pretty sneaky. Especially my mom. "I still think if there was a real treasure they would have done something about it, you know?"

I noticed my mom smile a little bit. Yeah, she was definitely listening in. It was kind of annoying, but we weren't talking about anything I didn't want her knowing. In fact, I kind of wanted her knowing everything for a while.

"Then why aren't you letting it go?" Logan flopped back in his raft, dipping his head into the water.

"I hate to agree with Logan, but, yeah—I mean we did recover that bag of gems." Noah gave me a weird look, like a bug flew up his nose or something. "That was a thing that happened. You were there."

"I *was* there. I remember it pretty clearly. I'm the one that got grounded over it, if you'll think back a minute or two." I looked up at the sky, but none of the birds or clouds seemed to have anything to offer. "We've been assuming it came from the museum.”

“Where else is it going to come from?” Logan scoffed and picked his head up. “Boston? New York City? Mars?”

“I mean, I guess it could have come from Mars. That one stone I kept was red.” Noah laughed for a second.

He stopped laughing when my mom jumped into the pool, pulled his float over, and got in his face. “That one stone you *what*?”

Noah had built up quite the tan over the summer, more of a tan than any hockey player had any business having, every bit of it faded away when my mom got that close to him with that look on her face.

I don’t blame him, honestly. One of my teachers once told me she makes men see their own graves.

“The rock I *would have kept*, if it wouldn’t have been wrong to keep it?” He squeaked the words out and forced a huge, cheesy smile onto his face. It didn’t fool anyone.

“Noah, relax. I’m not going to hurt you.” Mom took a deep breath. “But you have to tell the truth. Did you keep something from the evidence you turned over to Officer Cavan?”

Noah shook his head, but Logan wasn’t going to pass up an opportunity to get revenge for the beatdown Noah dealt him earlier. “He did. He totally did. It’s in his hockey bag.”

Noah whipped his head around to glare at his brother. “Dude. Shut. Up.”

“It’s right there, in the same pocket where he keeps his mouth guard.” Logan cackled with glee. “Want me to get it, Mrs. Cavan?”

Mom gave him the same look Noah had. "It's Ms. Corwin, thanks. And yes, please do. I'm not going poking around in hockey bags that don't belong to my kid." She shuddered and turned her attention back to Noah.

Mrs. McCrory had her phone out. "Should I give Fred a call?"

Noah started to shake.

Mom stared at him for a few seconds. "Better call Lt. Ramos instead. Fred's still on medical leave."

Noah slumped back onto his float. "Oh thank God."

Mrs. McCrory got up to make her call, and Logan scurried to go find his brother's treasure.

Mom relaxed a little bit, now that there was a plan. "Relax, Noah. You probably won't be in trouble. You're still a kid. It's possible that the gem you took could be the clue that solves the museum mystery once and for all. Wouldn't that be exciting?"

Noah seemed to fold in on himself. I'd never see a boy try to become origami before. It was kind of fun and kind of disturbing, all at the same time. "Look, can we not? I understand that it was wrong, and I shouldn't have done it. It was an impulse."

Mom's smile turned into a thin flat line. "Noah, we both know Logan's the impulsive one. You picked the gem for a reason. Do you want to tell me what it is, or do you want me to pull it out of your brother?"

"Do what you want to him, he already ratted me out." Noah scowled and looked away.

"Hm. So whatever it is you haven't told him yet." Mom tapped her jaw as she considered the problem in front of her.

He gasped. "What, are you psychic now or something?"

"Or something. He'll be back soon. You only have a few seconds to tell me what it was before he hears."

Noah went from bone white to scarlet in an instant. "IwasgonnagiveittoMallory." He said the words almost too fast to be understood.

Almost.

I only stopped myself from screaming by covering my mouth with my hands. I jumped off my float, swam as fast as I could to the nearest ladder, and climbed out of the pool. Once I was on dry land, I ran as fast as I could for the house and locked myself in the bathroom.

Once I was safe where no one could see me, I threw up. I know, it's gross, but so is the thought of Noah Scott giving me jewelry. Or *any* boys giving me jewelry, since we're being honest right now, although I do have a special little vial of spite for Noah.

What was he thinking? What had so shut his brain down that he thought it was a good idea to go pilfering evidence in a major crime to go giving me gems? I wasn't the princess type. The way to my heart was on the ice, not through the jewelry department. I didn't even own a dress!

And since when did Noah Freaking Scott want to go winning my heart or whatever in the first place?

I rinsed out my mouth and looked at myself in the mirror. I wasn't going to let any of this junk get to me. I had too much work to do to get all turned around by this . . . whatever it was. I was going to grow up and be a Bruin.

I threw my shoulders back, held my head high, and headed back outside. Noah's face was still scarlet, and he wouldn't even look at me. Logan had retrieved the gem, and he was showing it to Mom.

The gem was red, like a ruby. It was pretty, I guess, if you're into that sort of thing. It looked like the sort of thing Nan would have on a necklace or something. Mom was frowning at it though, which made me wonder. Maybe it was cursed?

She turned to Mrs. McCrory. "Sarah, can you take a look at this? I don't know a whole lot about gems."

Mrs. McCrory examined the stone carefully, and then her eyes widened. "Lil, this isn't a real gem at all. It's glass."

CHAPTER TWENTY-SIX

My own personal crisis would have to wait. We had bigger things on our plate than Noah's weird crush, which probably wasn't even really a crush. He just had a pressing urge to steal evidence and give it to me because I'm such a good winger. That's it. Nothing to puke about.

Lt. Ramos showed up and gave Mr. Snuffles a scritch. "Can't wait to have you back on the job, big guy."

Mr. Snuffles wagged his tail. Sure, he was enjoying his vacation, but he liked doing his job even more.

Mom and Mrs. McCrory showed him the fake ruby. They both minimized Noah's role in having it. They couldn't exactly deny he'd held onto it, but they didn't bring me into it at all. I promised myself I'd make Mom dinner for the next week if she could continue leaving me the heck out of that narrative.

I couldn't keep quiet though. Something seemed off, more than just Noah hanging onto this "ruby" just to give it to the best winger in the league.

(And okay, maybe my personal crisis wasn't taking as much of a back seat as I wanted it to.)

"There's something I still don't understand, Lt. Ramos. I mean, we gave you the whole bag of these things.

Didn't you examine them?"

He sighed and hung his head. "Honestly, we didn't do a deep analysis on them. Mr. Edwards positively identified the bag as being from the museum's collection, so we didn't need to waste the crime lab's resources on analysis." He sat down at the table. "I know it sounds lazy, but the fact is everyone uses the same crime lab—the state police crime lab. And they have to process the evidence from every crime in Massachusetts."

The other kids and I exchanged glances. "That doesn't sound like a great idea." Logan scratched his head. "I mean I don't know a lot about police stuff, just what I see on TV and what Mallory won't shut the heck up about—"

I punched him on the arm.

He continued like I hadn't done anything. "But there's a lot of crime in some places and, you know, not a lot in others. Places like Black Sail Bay don't have a lot of crime. It seems unfair to make us fight for space and time in the lab with places like Boston and Springfield, you know?"

Lt. Ramos nodded, a little grin on his face. "Well, you're not wrong. And it can be frustrating, believe me. The other side of that is that smaller towns like Black Sail Bay can't afford to have a proper crime lab. We don't have a ton of crime, but when we *do*, it wouldn't be fair to have our crimes go unsolved or have our criminals go free because we can't get testing. So there's a tradeoff, like there is with everything."

He set his hat down on the table. "The good news is that the bag of gems is still in the evidence locker. The case is still open, so it will stay there until the case is solved."

Mom frowned and leaned forward. "Forgive me. I'm not trying to interfere with your job, I'm legitimately asking as a museum board member. Has Dr. Edwards asked you in any way about the bag of gems?"

Lt. Ramos shook his head. "No, he hasn't checked in with us at all. I thought that was a little odd, but with everything going on with the Cranston gang, I had more pressing issues on my mind." He muttered something in Spanish and glanced at me guiltily. "Sorry, excuse me. You think he's dirty, don't you?"

Mom sat up straight again. "I certainly don't want to open myself to charges of spreading false accusations." She placed a hand on her chest. "I just think it's interesting that he claims the gems were in the museum's collection, but isn't interested in retrieving such valuable artifacts. Lt. Ramos, there are no precious gems in the museum's catalog, whether in storage or on display. Black Sail Bay was founded by Puritans. They had no use for that type of display and, in fact, would have come down hard on anyone who wore it."

Mrs. McCrory tipped her head to the side. "What about pirates though? Isn't that the whole idea behind changing the name of the town? There were so many pirates making themselves at home here that they changed the name of the town."

Mom rolled her eyes. "They were still outlaws. They had to at least pretend to fit in with the local populace. The colonial authorities couldn't fail to notice a bunch of men running around sporting massive rubies and emeralds, could they?"

"It would stand out today too." Lt. Ramos chuckled. "You're absolutely sure the museum has never had anything like this in its possession?"

Mom sighed, shoulders slumping. "Director Edwards has been . . . lackadaisical with his record keeping. It's an issue. But he's also dealing with a very small budget, all things considered. He wouldn't have been able to afford to purchase something so expensive without coming to us for an extra appropriation, which we couldn't have given him. And, yes, he'd have publicized the heck out of it."

My brain finally made the connection. "You think he staged the whole thing."

Mom put her hand on her chest. "I didn't accuse him of anything. I just pointed out some relevant facts."

"Isn't that how you caught me lying about who broke the window at Mr. Cavan's house?" Noah spoke up, finally.

Mom winked at him. Noah just gaped.

Lt. Ramos chuckled, but there was a sadness to his eyes that hadn't been there before. "I'm going to need to talk to the captain. And, I think, a judge." He reached into his pocket and pulled out a small plastic bag. "Thanks for coming clean, Noah. I'm going to have to tell my superiors what you did, but I don't think you're going to be in trouble. You admitted what you did voluntarily and you're still a kid, so I don't see a need to prosecute. Plus, what you did might have just solved a case for us." He ruffled Noah's damp hair.

Mom put a protective arm around Noah's shoulders. "Be sure to let me or Clara know if that changes. We'll be sure he's taken care of."

Lt. Ramos smiled at her. "No one better to do it." He stood up and left the patio.

Noah turned to Mom. "What did you mean by

that?"

Mom patted the seat next to her—my seat, usually, except I was standing behind her. "Noah, you withheld evidence from a known felony investigation. That's normally a pretty big deal. Now, Lt. Ramos doesn't want to see you charged for it, and I don't think the chief of police would either. I don't want to scare you, but I do need you to know that what you did is pretty serious. If the chief feels strongly about it, and overrules Lt. Ramos, you're going to need an attorney. They can't legally question you without one, or your parent. As it happens, I'm still technically a member of the Bar and my sister's also a lawyer. We're not going to let anything happen to you, okay?"

Noah's eyes were as big as two plates. He nodded slowly.

I felt bad for him, even if the reason he'd done the thing in the first place made me want to crawl right out of my skin. "Hey, if the chief overrules Lt. Ramos you can always make Logan go to jail in your place."

"Hey!" Logan squawked in outrage.

We almost couldn't hear him over how loud everyone was laughing.

"And that's the end of you reading Dickens. He's giving you ideas." Mom didn't mean it. I knew *that* much, just from the way she was doubled over with laughter.

None of us felt much like fooling around anymore, but we did get back into the pool and lounge around until Mr. Scott showed up to pick the boys up. Mom disappeared with him for a little while, I assume so she could tell him about Noah's terrible idea and the results. Mr. Scott looked pale when they emerged, but he didn't say anything else about it. He just loaded the twins and their hockey bags into his car and took them home.

Mom and I headed home afterward. She waited until we were home and on our own ground to spring her question on me. "You want to talk about it?"

"About?" Honestly, she could have meant anything. She could have been talking about the resolution to the museum theft, or the possibility of our team's best center facing legal trouble. She could have been talking about the whole mess with the Cranston gang.

She wasn't.

"The thing with Noah. His little crush." She led me into the kitchen and started pulling dinner together. "I saw you turn green and make a beeline for the bathroom."

"Maybe I just had to pee." I crossed my arms over my chest, but I couldn't meet her eyes. I never could lie to Mom.

"It's okay to not be interested, Mallory." She gave me a gentle smile and pulled some salad greens from the fridge. "His interest doesn't require anything from you."

"It's still gross." I made a face. I didn't know I was shrinking in on myself until my shoulders hurt.

"Well, sure. Some people your age might be starting to feel crushes, but not all. You're still young, and your love of hockey takes up pretty much all of your time. That's fine. There is absolutely nothing wrong with that." She started chopping up some chicken. "It can feel like a lot of people are starting to get into that kind of thing, but seriously, you'll feel it when you're ready and not one minute before. Don't fake it because you feel obligated or left behind. That's just cruel to you and to the other person."

I nodded, relaxing my shoulders a little. "You make it sound so sensible."

"That's because I've lived through it. The benefit of having a mother is she gets to make all the mistakes so you don't have to." She laughed and passed me some cheese. "In all seriousness, Mal, you're a good kid. You've got a great head on your shoulders and I trust you, but sometimes it's good to get a little reinforcement, right? There's a lot going on right now, and everything's been super intense.

"This whole thing with the Cranston gang? That's not normal. It's not something most adults have to deal with, and it's super not normal for a bunch of eleven-year-olds. It's okay to be freaked out. It's okay to feel unsafe. It's okay to be a little unsteady for a while. And if you have a really strong reaction to something that would normally just make you say, 'Ew, gross,' that's okay too."

"You really are psychic." I remembered what Noah had said to her by the pool.

"Just paying attention, sweetheart. And remember, I've seen stuff like this happen before." She wrapped her arms around me. "I love you more than anything in the world, Mallory. And I'm beyond proud of you. You can't even imagine. It's okay to sit back, rest, and let the grown-ups handle things for a while."

I nodded, but I couldn't help but ask. "I want to stick with it though. Like, we wouldn't have found out about the gems being fake if I hadn't still wanted to find the stupid treasure or figure out the museum case, right? I knew something was still unfinished. I think it's going to keep bothering me."

"I think this whole mess is going to keep bothering

all of us for a while, but fair enough." She kissed the top of my head. "I'll see what we can do."

CHAPTER TWENTY-SEVEN

I don't know what strings Mom pulled. They must have been pretty big though, and she must have pulled them tight as heck because the day after we found out about the gem being fake we all went to the museum after hockey camp.

The boys complained. Okay, most of the vocal complaining came from Logan. Noah mostly sat uncomfortably in his seat with a face as white as center ice, every muscle in his body tense enough to bounce quarters off.

It was Logan who rolled his eyes and huffed. "Dude, we just *went* to the museum. Considering that nothing has changed there in fifty years, I'm pretty sure we've seen enough of it to last until we're old dried husks. Can't we just go home and play video games? We could write a video game about Black Sail Bay, and it would be better than the stupid museum."

I turned in my seat to give him the death glare Mom couldn't. "Dude, are you kidding? You can't write with a pen and paper, in English. You can't write a video game."

Noah almost looked like he could laugh. Maybe, if

he wasn't so afraid of my mom, he'd have actually done it. I felt bad for him, just a little.

"I can learn." Logan sniffed. "There's an online class my dad found. And hey—you can learn. We can both take the class and see which one of us makes the best game. And then we can *sell* the game, and I'll make a trillion dollars, I'll buy this whole stupid town, and I'll buy that dog right out from under you. See if I don't."

Mr. Snuffles growled from the back of the wagon.

I had been about to shout something mean, but Mr. Snuffles reminded me how ridiculous Logan's statement was. "Um, you do know they don't sell police dogs, right?"

"One. Trillion. Dollars." Logan crossed his arms over his chest and looked smug.

I just shook my head and looked out the window. I'd never had much interest in programming before, but if Logan thought he could do it better than me, he had another thing coming. Logan thought homework was a four-letter word, and he tried to spell it with four letters too. I'd find that class, and I'd kick his scrawny butt.

Mom just grinned and shook her head.

We pulled into her "director" parking spot at the museum. Lt. Ramos met us in full uniform at the front door, his jaw set hard. I'd never seen him look like this before.

I turned to look around. The police cars weren't marked, but I'd spent half of my actual life at the police station. I knew every one of those cars and most of the guys in them.

I gulped. "Do you really think it's going to go that badly?"

210

His gaze snapped over to Mom, who sighed.

"Probably not. Dr. Edwards is more of a coward and a sneak than the kind of guy who comes out guns blazing. Still, he's probably going to be feeling desperate when he sees Lt. Ramos walk in, and desperate people can be a little unpredictable."

"We wouldn't have let you kids be here at all if we thought he was likely to be violent, but things have a way of going south when you least expect it." Lt. Ramos' lips tightened. "If you hear an order, you follow it. You do not ask questions. You do not say a word. You do not look back. You do what you're told and you do it fast. Are we clear?"

All four of us nodded. "Yes, sir." Noah looked down at the floor and swayed a little bit on his feet. I wondered if he was going to pass out.

We walked into the museum. I felt a little bit like I did before a big game, marching out of the locker room with my team. And this really was my team, I guess. Noah and Logan were literally my team. Viv might not play hockey, but she'd been by my side in every other way since we were old enough to recognize other kids. My mom had always been my biggest supporter—the most important part of my defensive line, really. And Lt. Ramos—well, he might not be part of the team most of the time, but he'd been right there with us the whole time. He'd earned his sweater.

Everything sense was sharper, again just like it was before a game. Our footsteps echoed, weirdly in time with Lt. Ramos', against the cement floor. The lights were brighter, the air-conditioning louder.

And, because we'd just come from hockey, we

stank.

We marched through the exhibits straight to the stairs. I noticed, through the corner of my eye, that one of the officers with us used some kind of key to shut the elevator down. Hopefully, there wasn't anyone inside; that would be terrifying. I got why they had to do it, but still.

The administrative offices were in the back, beyond a big frosted-glass door marked "Administration: Employees Only." Mom had a key card, so we didn't have to knock.

I had expected something big and exciting. Maybe a whole team of designers, archaeologists, and historians, doing their best with a limited budget to bring us the best possible historical experience. Maybe I visualized a couple of accountants in a corner, fighting with pages of receipts and bills.

What I found was one assistant at a decrepit desk, covered in papers, arguing with someone on the phone. She was older, maybe Nan's age, and sounded like she'd been smoking cigarettes since before she was my age. "Look, I understand the bills are past due, but they're also incorrect." She held up a finger as she continued to argue with the person on the phone. "I respect your position, but we never agreed to pay a finance charge."

Mom just sighed and walked past her, leading the charge toward Dr. Edwards' office. We knew it was his because his name was on the sign.

Dr. Edwards was a thin man with a face like a weasel. He was probably in his fifties. He wore a tan suit with a pink shirt. I thought he'd probably chosen the shirt without trying it on, because it made his skin look yellow. He had a big bald spot on the top of his head, and yellow teeth. "Agnes, I'm pretty sure I told you not to—" He stopped. "Director Corwin. I apologize. I wasn't aware we had an appointment."

Then he noticed the rest of us, and Lt. Ramos. He sighed and pursed his lips. "Look, Director, I'm grateful for the publicity your daughter and her friends brought to the museum with their discovery. But it's not appropriate to just stop everything and pad up children's' egos every time they're feeling a little down, especially not at their age. It's not good for them."

All four of us gaped at him. Was that seriously how he thought of us?

Lt. Ramos cleared his throat. "This isn't about children's egos, Dr. Edwards. Do you remember the bag of gems the children found?"

Edwards waved his bony hand. "Yes, of course. It was in newspapers all over the country. How could I forget? And of course they had that whole mess with those Rhode Island drug dealers. You could hardly escape the news." He rolled his eyes. "If you ask me, you've created monsters. They've gotten addicted to press coverage. Good luck breaking them of *that* habit."

Noah started toward him, fists clenched. I threw my arm over his chest as a barrier, without ever tearing my eyes from the museum director. He had a lot of dismissive words, but a bead of sweat trickled down from his temple.

Even though the temperature in his office was almost as cold as the temperature at the rink.

"It's interesting you mention that." Ramos nodded, just as calm and controlled as ever. "You know, it's also interesting you spoke about *the publicity Mallory and her friends brought to the museum* instead of how they found something that belonged to the museum. And while we're on the subject, it's interesting that you never put these so-called pirate treasures on display for the public, or inquired about their status after they were recovered."

Edwards lost some of his color, but he leaned back in his seat and shook his head. "I was trying not to make more work for you while you kept the brats out of trouble. Guess a good deed never goes unpunished."

"Give it a break." Mom snorted. "You know there were never any gems in inventory."

Edwards shrugged. "So we're a little backed up on paperwork."

Mom chuckled. "No. If you'd had actual treasure, you'd have lost no time displaying it. I noticed you didn't hesitate to exploit the kids' discovery or their bravery in coming forward. Admissions are triple what they were last year, and it's only July. Agnes wasn't trying to push off vendors with 'We don't have money,' she was fighting over terms."

"We've been very fortunate. Maybe you can finally afford to hire some help next year."

"Except less than half of that money has made it into the bank account." Lt. Ramos smirked.

Edwards flushed scarlet with rage. "You need a warrant for that!"

"Actually he doesn't. As a director, I have visibility into the museum's finances. And the board of directors can launch our own audit at any time, should we so choose. Which we did—*before any of this started.*"

"Hands where I can see them." Lt. Ramos finally pulled his handcuffs out. "You have the right to remain silent. Anything you say can be used against you in court.

You have the right to have an attorney present during questioning. If you can't afford an attorney, one will be provided for you."

Edwards obeyed, but while he did he opened and closed his mouth a bunch of times. He looked like a fish stranded on the beach at low tide. I wasn't throwing this one back out into the water though.

"You can't arrest me! I've tripled our revenue. I *improved* things, and not just for the museum but for the whole town. Tourism is up for all of Black Sail Bay. Every hotel, motel, and bed-and-breakfast in the area is in the black this year. Every restaurant. Every attraction. And it's all because of me."

"It's all because of these kids, John." Lt. Ramos cuffed Dr. Edwards' hands behind his back. "People don't care about the museum. They care about these kids finding the 'treasure.' They care about these kids standing up to a bunch of drug dealers—and by the way, did you have anything to do with that?"

Edwards recoiled, as best as he could with his hands cuffed behind him. "Don't be absurd. Drug gangs decrease tourism. They might have used the publicity around pirate treasures to hide their activity, digging in the dirt and such to make their drops, but I'd never associate with the likes of them."

Ramos shrugged. "Keep up that attitude in the pen. It'll be fun. We'll investigate your claims, obviously, but for now the charges are just fraud and embezzlement." He frog-marched Edwards down the stairs and out the door.

A crowd had arrived outside the museum, to include a few reporters. I don't know how they heard about anything that was going on or how they got there so quickly. Either way, they got a lot of pictures of the museum curator being led out in handcuffs, and of the five of us coming out behind him in a line. Black Sail Bay Police had an official spokeswoman there to answer questions, and that was it.

The whole thing was over.

CHAPTER TWENTY-EIGHT

Camp wound down by the middle of August. We had a big tournament against some of the other hockey camps in the Boston area. I was pretty happy with how we played, especially since we took first place.

I was twice as happy to hear someone from that Braintree hockey camp warn a defenseman away from me. "Don't mess with her, I saw her on TV. She beat up a drug dealer who had a knife. Stay away from her center too—he's shady."

I told Mom and Dad about it. Mom laughed. Dad cringed, but I could see a little smile playing around the corners of his mouth.

Mom and Dad both took me on a vacation after hockey camp let out. It was a little weird going somewhere with both of them, but Dad was on medical leave and they both agreed I'd had a stressful summer. A little time someplace safe and mellow would be just what the doctor ordered.

We went to California. We spent a little time at Disneyland and a little time in San Diego. I loved both places. We did some hiking in San Diego that truly took my breath away, and I learned some wild things about the area. There was so much more than surfing and a zoo.

Of course, surfing and the zoo were fun too.

When we got back, Dr. Edwards was ready to go to court.

He'd agreed to plead guilty. Dad said it was because they had him "dead to rights." Mom said it was because his wife, the elementary school principal, made him. I didn't know what to believe, and I didn't care. Dr. Edwards had confessed, right in front of us all, and he was guilty. I didn't care why he wasn't going to fight it in court.

I begged Mom and Dad to let me be there for Dr. Edwards' day in court. They agreed eventually. It was weird. I had to dress up, which Dad said meant I had to wear a dress. Mom found me a nice pantsuit to wear while Dad and I had a screaming match about it, and I wore that while I sat beside her.

Mr. Snuffles, as always, sat by my feet. I think he'd have liked to sit on the bench beside me, but that gets frowned on in court. Even for police dogs.

Dr. Edwards went through his confession. It wasn't anything I hadn't heard before, although he sounded more ashamed of himself and less like a cartoon villain this time. The judge sentenced him to five years in the state penitentiary, which didn't sound like a whole lot to me.

I figured that would be it, but a pretty Black woman with a camera crew behind her approached. She introduced herself as Tamika Jones from some big national news network I'd never thought much about before, and asked if she could interview me now that the cases were closed.

I thought about it. Dad looked like he was going to blow six fuses right then and there, but Mom winked at me.

"I don't mind," I said after a minute, "but can you interview all of us? The other kids too, I mean. It wasn't just me. Viv did just as much, and so did Noah and I guess Logan too."

She grinned at me. "That seems reasonable. Mrs. Cavan—"

"Ms. Corwin," my mom and dad said at the same time.

"Ms. Corwin, can I ask for your help in setting the interview up?"

It only took a couple of hours to pull everyone together in Mom's backyard. Not only did we get Viv and the Scott twins, but we got Lt. Ramos too. I felt better about the whole interview now that he was here, and I could see by the way that Dad's freak-out meter lowered that he did too.

Ms. Jones asked us a few general questions about ourselves first. They were pretty basic—what did we like to do in school, were we big sports fans, that kind of thing. Then she asked about the case—how had we gotten involved, wasn't it kind of scary when we had these guys coming after us, what did we do when these scary grown-ups came after us in places we were used to?

So Noah told her the story about the one guy coming after him in the pizza parlor, which led to Viv talking about when the other guy trying to break into her house. Ms. Jones winced at both stories. "It sounds like Mallory's the one you both turned to."

"Well, yeah. Her dad's a cop, and her mom writes murder mysteries. So she always knows stuff we don't, stuff about how to stay safe. She's also not scared of anything—

ever." Noah turned bright red. "I admit I panicked. I should have called 9-1-1 when I was locked in that bathroom, but I called Mal. It was what I'd do if I was in trouble on the ice, so it's what I kind of reverted to."

Now, it was my turn to blush. "I guess I'm a little more used to hearing about some scary stuff, just because of who my parents are." I picked at the seam on my new suit. "Viv's dad's a doctor, so if I've got a question about getting sick or an injury or something I usually call her, right? But yeah—we're teammates. We're supposed to have each other's back."

Ms. Jones gave me a gentle smile. "Do you all believe it was just a coincidence that the dealers and Dr. Edwards happened to do their crimes at the same time?"

We all squirmed. Logan scratched his head.

Finally, Lt. Ramos intervened. "The dealers had been doing their business all over the North Shore for a while, ma'am. Their link in Black Sail Bay was Steve, who worked at the rink. He's the one who came up with the idea of burying their drops—the drug shipments and the payments—to take advantage of old legends about pirate treasure.

"Dr. Edwards was desperate to keep a job that let him golf when he wanted, schmooze with donors, and feel superior to other people. He'd never have voluntarily talked to a bunch of guys like this gang from Cranston, and they'd never have spoken to him. They were middlemen."

"I see." Jones nodded like that made any sense at all to her.

I'm glad it worked for someone, because it was all a little more complex than I was ready to follow right now.

Then she turned back to us kids. "So, this all started

because of supposed pirate treasure. How are you doing, now that you know there's no pirate treasure here in Black Sail Bay?"

We all stared at her. You could have heard a pin drop. Then I laughed. I couldn't have helped it. Viv picked it up next, and then Logan. Even Noah, who was still nervous after the whole thing with the fake gem he'd kept back, had to join in.

"Ma'am, the great thing about pirate treasure is that it's always there," I told her. "It's just waiting in the next spot you look."

"Or maybe the one after that." Viv's grin was wide, manic as she slung an arm over my shoulder.

"I was kind of upset at first. Finding a heap of treasure would solve a lot of problems." Noah ran a hand through his hair and gave a sheepish grin. "But Mallory's right. We can't prove that pirates ever buried treasure in Black Sail Bay, and the fact is that they probably didn't. The point is, *they might have*. You never know."

Logan jumped in, nodding his head so fast he looked like a basketball bouncing. "You could be doing home repairs and find treasure hidden in the walls. You could be trying to put in a new swimming pool and find a chest full of gold doubloons. You could be running through the woods and trip on a sack of gems that leads you on an adventure like you've never thought of before."

I grinned. "And that's another thing. Lt. Ramos, how much money was in that Tupperware we found?"

He blinked. "Maybe a hundred grand?"

"That's a pretty big treasure as far as I'm concerned." I hadn't thought about it in quite this way until I said it, but now I could see it so clearly. "We didn't get to keep it, and we had a lot of scary moments because of it, but it was absolutely a treasure. And while we try to make pirates out to be these great, noble guys, a lot of them were just your garden variety jerks. Some drug dealers are probably kind of noble, but a lot of them do a lot of bad stuff too.

"So in a way, we did find pirate treasure. And who knows how often they used that system to make their deals? How many more Tupperware are there out there?"

Ms. Jones was watching me with huge eyes, her mouth a perfectly round O. "So you think people should still come to Black Sail Bay for the pirates?"

"Sure." Viv shrugged. "And the pretty beaches and the great food and our absolutely kick-butt youth hockey team that just won first place in the summer tournament." We all high-fived each other, and Noah picked up the story.

"I know a lot of people are probably disappointed by how things turned out, but what Dr. Edwards did doesn't really change anything for Black Sail Bay. This town has always been here, it's always going to be here, and there's always going to be cool stuff to find. It doesn't matter who's running the museum."

She shook hands with all of us, eyes gleaming. "That was great. You kids are definitely going places, that's for sure."

Dad put a hand on my back. "In a few years, definitely. For now, I think they only place they're going is out for pizza."

Mr. Snuffles barked, tail thumping against the floor.

"You've got his vote!" Ms. Jones laughed.